"So what do we do now?" Arlie asked *uncertainly. "Should I change into something more comfortable or just strip down?"*

"Whoa." Dan laughed. "Slow down. I suppose we should begin by getting used to touching each other."

"Okay, I'm game. What do you want to touch?"

"Come here, idiot," he said, drawing her back against him. Slowly he pulled the pins from her hair, letting it fall around her shoulders, and began to stroke the mass of ebony silk.

Arlie sighed and relaxed against him, waiting. But he simply continued to touch her hair softly and slowly. "This is very nice," she said, "but you've been patting me on the head since I was six years old. When do we get to the good stuff?"

"Arlie, you fiend," Dan said through clenched teeth, pushing her back onto the bed and leaning over to grasp her shoulders. "How am I supposed to seduce you if you're going to sit there critiquing my performance? There should be a law against making love to your best friend. . . ."

WHAT ARE *LOVESWEPT* ROMANCES?

They are stories of true romance and touching emotion. We believe those two very important ingredients are constants in our highly sensual and very believable stories in the *LOVESWEPT* line. Our goal is to give you, the reader, stories of consistently high quality that may sometimes make you laugh, sometimes make you cry, but are always fresh and creative and contain many delightful surprises within their pages.

Most romance fans read an enormous number of books. Those they truly love, they keep. Others may be traded with friends and soon forgotten. We hope that each *LOVESWEPT* romance will be a treasure—a "keeper." We will always try to publish

LOVE STORIES YOU'LL NEVER FORGET
BY AUTHORS YOU'LL ALWAYS REMEMBER

The Editors

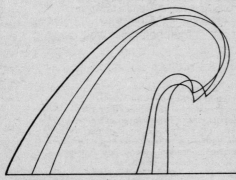

LOVESWEPT • 26

Billie Green

Once in a Blue Moon

BANTAM BOOKS
NEW YORK • TORONTO • LONDON • SYDNEY • AUCKLAND

ONCE IN A BLUE MOON

A Bantam Book / December 1983

*LOVESWEPT® and the wave device are registered
trademarks of Bantam Books, a division of
Bantam Doubleday Dell Publishing Group, Inc.
Registered in U.S. Patent
and Trademark Office and elsewhere.*

*If you would be interested in receiving protective vinyl
covers for your Loveswept books, please write to this address
for information:*

> *Loveswept
> Bantam Books
> P.O. Box 985
> Hicksville, NY 11802*

ISBN 0-553-21631-7

Published simultaneously in the United States and Canada

*Bantam Books are published by Bantam Books, a division
of Bantam Doubleday Dell Publishing Group, Inc. Its trademark, consisting of the words "Bantam Books" and the
portrayal of a rooster, is Registered in U.S. Patent and
Trademark Office and in other countries. Marca Registrada.
Bantam Books, 666 Fifth Avenue, New York, New York 10103.*

One

She was back. Really back. The bird she heard singing in the drooping willow tree across the street wasn't a sophisticated French bird. It was a down-home, cacophonous Texas bird. And the afternoon sun, whose rays penetrated her clothing and all the way to the center of her body, wasn't the discreet European sun. It was a gaudy, larger-than-life Texas sun.

Arlie leaned back against the wooden porch column and took a deep breath, laughing in pure joy as the air seared her nostrils. She shifted her position on her makeshift stool, trying to keep the metal clasp of her suitcase from digging into her linen-covered derriere and flexed her pained feet in the confining leather shoes.

As she checked her watch for the fifth time in ten minutes, she heard the faint purr of a car in the distance. Involuntarily straightening her back, she turned her head expectantly toward the sound. Her long, sleek ponytail caught the bright sun and sparkled momentarily with a vibrant rainbow of colors before settling down to lustrous black as she watched the car pass.

Leaning forward in disappointment, she rested her chin in the palms of her hands. Arlie had been traveling since early the day before and ached for a bath and bed. Her linen slacks and open-necked shirt, both showing the effects of her long trip, felt grubby, but as she turned her face to catch a cooling breeze, the radiant vitality in her lightly tanned face would have fooled most people into thinking her cool and fresh. She flexed her toes again and wondered for the hundredth time how on earth she was going to explain about Stephan.

Arlie sighed and put the worry away, glancing up to see an attractive older woman in a pink satin jogging suit walk out of the white brick townhouse across the street. She was holding the leash of a beautifully coiffed poodle in a matching pink outfit. Dan had evidently come up in the world, she thought, stifling a giggle. The last time she had landed on his doorstep, he had been living in a tiny one bedroom apartment with boisterous, friendly neighbors. This street of beautifully landscaped townhouses, although obviously housing the affluent, had the same welcoming warmth. Or maybe it was simply that Arlie knew she was home at last and she was transferring her joy to the immediate scene around her.

But deep down she knew that home didn't change no matter how many years had passed. The explosive growth she had seen on her trip from the airport hadn't been able to disguise the warmth that still lay beneath the cosmopolitan veneer of the city of Fort Worth. It reached out to her and embraced her exuberantly.

And Arlie also knew that the elegant structure behind her couldn't change Dan. He was always there when she needed him and had been since she was six years old and he was fourteen, though he'd seemed much more than eight years her senior. It had been three years now since she had last run to Dan for help. Three exciting, confusing, and sometimes lonely years. But now Arlie was back and once more she was waiting for Dan to pull her out of a scrape as he had that first time so long ago.

The sound of another car brought her head up and a slow smile spread across her full lips, her wide set violet eyes shining with anticipation. She didn't stand or try to straighten her travel-rumpled clothing when she recognized his red hair through the windshield of the white Lincoln.

The car slid to a stop and a large man swung out of the driver's side. Arlie scarcely noticed the woman sitting in the front seat of the car. Her eyes were glued to the man as he walked slowly around the front of the car and up the walk toward her.

Three years had wrought changes, of course. The quiet inner strength he had always possessed had spread to the outside. The awkward angularity was gone and sometime during those three years his breadth had finally caught up with his height, giving his frame a solid, symmetrical beauty. His outrageously red hair had darkened to a blazing auburn, but she was delighted to note that it still refused to be tamed. It framed his face in an unruly tangle of thick, springy curls. Other than being fuller and more rugged, his face hadn't been changed much. He was still not handsome. To the casual observer he might even have seemed plain, but not to Arlie as she watched his slow approach. His dear, familiar face was the most beautiful thing she had seen in three years.

He stopped several feet from her, a crooked smile spreading across his face—and now the casual observer would have wondered how she could ever have thought him plain.

"So trouble's back," he said softly.

Arlie was up off her suitcase and into his waiting arms before he drew another breath. "Daniel," was all she could manage to say as she pressed her face into his broad chest.

Grasping her shoulders, he held her away from him to look into her face. She met his searching eyes and words were unnecessary. For long moments they simply stood there reading the years— the pain, the growth—in each other's eyes.

Then a delicate cough brought them back to the present and Dan turned to the small blonde woman standing behind him on the sidewalk. Arlie looked at the petite woman curiously. She was fashionably dressed, thirty-ish and extremely attractive.

"Diane," he said as though suddenly recalling her presence. "Diane, I'd like you to meet the bane of my life. My own personal albatross. The devilish thorn in my tender side. Every time I get complacent and think my life is running smoothly, she pops up to disrupt things completely." He glanced at Arlie and caught her unrepentant grin. "This is Arlie Fleming. Arlie, this is Diane Prescott, a very dear friend."

"Arlie Fleming?" the small woman asked before Arlie could acknowledge the introduction. "I've heard that name. In fact, I could swear I've seen you before."

"Oh, Arlie's famous. Or rather, *infamous*," Dan said, eyeing Arlie sternly as she looked carefully away from his disapproving stare. "You're probably thinking of the last of her adventures. It involved an actor, a count, and a bellhop."

"He was the manager of the hotel," Arlie corrected. "And you needn't sound like I was responsible for the incident. I just happened to be there." Arlie smiled innocently at Diane, her eyes dancing with amusement. "Just because I got into a few scrapes when I was a child, Dan always assumes these things are my fault. I'm simply unlucky. A victim of circumstances."

"You're a five-foot-six-inch stick of dynamite," Dan muttered, turning to Diane. "Do you know what they used to call us? The devil and Daniel Webster."

Diane laughed at Dan's disgruntled face and Arlie's feigned innocence. "I want to hear all about it, but don't you think we should go inside?"

As they moved to the porch, Dan hesitated momentarily and gave Arlie a questioning look when he saw her luggage, but stooped to pick up the largest suitcase without speaking, then unlocked the front door. They stepped into a small tiled entry hall and Dan motioned them into an old-fashioned, spacious living room with a small brick fireplace and comfortably eclectic furnishings.

After Diane and Arlie had seated themselves on the couch, Dan leaned against the fireplace, one foot raised to rest on the hearth, and lit his pipe. He watched silently, a look of dry humor touching his rugged face, as Diane began to question Arlie.

"When did you meet Dan?" she asked in her soft, musical voice.

"When I was six years old." Arlie leaned back and sighed, her brow wrinkled in thought. "I was a fugitive from justice, hiding in the shrubbery beside his house. When he hauled me out I thought he was the truant officer. I wasn't going to give myself up gracefully, so our meeting was a little rough."

"A little rough?" Dan interrupted. "You came out biting and kicking like the little wildcat you were. I limped for weeks after that."

"You should have identified yourself," Arlie replied righteously. "Anyway, he talked me into giving myself up. Which was a bad move, of course. I not only had to go back to school, but my father confined me to my room for a week. The first thing I did when I was paroled was to track down the fink who had caused my downfall. I think drawing and quartering was what I had in mind, but once again he made me talk out my anger and from then on whenever I had a problem, I went to Dan."

"Couldn't you have gone to your parents?"

"My mother died when I was born and somehow my father and I could never get on the same wavelength. He had wanted a daughter who would be a carbon copy of my mother. All sweet and demure and pretty. What he got was a bad-tempered tomboy with a loud mouth and scabby knees. I think he could have forgiven me my knees, but he could never forget that my mother had died giving birth to me. So he sent me to live with my aunt—and she promptly sent me back." Arlie shook her head regretfully. "It's the sad truth, but no one really appreciates scabby knees."

"It wasn't your knees, imp," Dan said smiling. "If I remember correctly, you told me you put Herman in her sewing box."

"Herman?" Diane asked.

"My hamster," Arlie explained. "I know it was very bad of me, but she had made a hurtful remark about my mother, and a five year old can be very vindictive. She said it was a good thing my mother hadn't lived to see what a horror I had grown into. I retaliated by putting Herman in her sewing box. I regretted it afterward, of course." Arlie's violet-blue eyes sparkled suddenly. "Ah, but you should have seen the look on her face when she reached in for navy blue worsted and found Herman instead."

Diane's laughter combined with Dan's deep chuckle.

"And it was after you returned home that you met Dan?" Diane asked.

"Yes. We lived in a small town south of Fort Worth and it was my first year at school. They made me wear dresses and shoes. Needless to say, I hated it. And in those days the girls were expected to play nice little girl games while the boys had fun. So I left. I was going to walk to Houston and become an astronaut."

"And Dan stopped you?"

"I managed to convince her that they wouldn't accept uneducated astronauts," Dan said, laughing softly at the memory.

"Yes, you traitor," Arlie said, looking at Dan reproachfully. "For a while I studied harder than any first grader in history, but it didn't last long. Before the month was out I had decided to become the first woman big league baseball player. And no one could convince me that you have to spell to be able to hit a ball."

Dan moved to lay his pipe in an ashtray and reclined in a wide leather chair. "That was the week I had to talk Old Man Hawkins out of skinning you alive for breaking his bedroom window."

"And that was the beginning of our long and happy association," Arlie said, grinning impudently. "We made a perfect pair. I got into trouble and Dan got me out of it. After he helped me the first time there was no backing out. He was my guardian angel whether he liked it or not."

"Until you married?" Diane asked.

Arlie glanced down at the carpet to avoid the look in Dan's suddenly narrowed eyes. "Yes," she said quietly, then turned her head to smile at Diane, her nose wrinkling in an irresistibly tomboyish way. "So you read about that fiasco in St. Moritz?"

Diane took the bait and began to ask eager questions about the places Arlie had been and the people she had met in the last three years. Arlie regaled her with all the latest gossip—some of it highly embroidered—about the beautiful people, her dark eyes twinkling with mischief as she willfully tore apart the reputations of the rich and famous. She was in the middle of describing a farcical, therefore hilarious, triangle involving one of Diane's favorite singers when the doorbell rang.

"Oh, no," Diane sighed in dismay. "That has to be Eric and he couldn't have come for me at a less opportune time." She clasped Arlie's hand. "Promise you'll tell me the rest later?"

"I promise." Arlie laughed as Diane rose to answer the door, then began to whistle softly to herself as she caught the vengeful gleam in Dan's eyes.

"Arlie, you demon," he whispered as Diane left the room. "How much of that did you make up?"

"Most of it," she said complacently. "Who's Eric?"

"Diane's brother," he said in exasperation. "How am I supposed to explain your warped sense of humor to Diane?"

Before she could reply, Diane returned, accompanied by an attractive blond man with laughing blue eyes.

"Arlie, this gorgeous hunk is my brother, Eric," Diane said, pulling him forward.

"Hello, Eric," Arlie said, extending her hand. Hunk was an understatement. He wore his casual shirt open at the throat, exposing smooth, tanned flesh. And the faded Levi's hugged his trim hips and muscular thighs like a second skin. Arlie looked up to find Eric was giving her the same close examination. Her mouth lifted in a smile as his curious gaze lingered on her full lips.

"Hel—*lo*, Arlie," he said softly, retaining his hold on her hand, his eyebrows raised in surprise.

"I thought you two had a family thing you had to go to?" Dan's voice was strangely stiff as he broke into the threads of empathy that were being spun between Arlie and Eric.

"It's not actually a family affair," Diane said. "But Mother insists it's necessary that we both attend." She then began a detailed explanation of why the formal dinner was so important.

"Have dinner with me tomorrow," Eric murmured under the cover of Diane's explanation, his blue eyes glinting with interest.

"Thank you. I'd like that," Arlie replied softly, smiling as she felt the waves of understanding flow between them. She recognized him immediately as a kindred spirit. She knew without question that the vitality and love of life she saw in Eric's eyes were reflected in her own. It would be nice to be with someone who shared her irrepressible, and slightly irreverent, sense of humor again. Now that Stephan . . .

"Arlie." Dan's voice was impatient, as though he had tried more than once to get her attention.

"I'm sorry," she said, looking up to find his brown eyes narrow and suspicious. "Did you say something?"

"I said Diane and Eric have to leave now."

Arlie walked to the door with Dan to see them out. As he left, Eric pressed her hand firmly and asked, "Is seven-thirty all right?"

"Seven-thirty is fine," she replied, avoiding Dan's eyes.

Turning away immediately as the door closed, she began to walk back into the living room only to have her arm grasped roughly, halting her steps. She glanced back over her shoulder, giving Dan an innocently questioning look.

"You can cut out the act, Arlie. This is me, remember? Now what in the hell have you done with your husband?"

Two

"Done with him?" Arlie asked, laughing. "You make it sound like I murdered him."

"I admit it crossed my mind lugging in your three-ton suitcase that it could contain his dismembered body! Frankly, though, I've always thought he would commit suicide in sheer exasperation before you could carry out any plans to murder him."

"You can set your mind at ease." She walked into the living room and took off her shoes, rubbing the bottoms of her aching feet on the carpet. "Ooh, that feels good." Turning to see him still standing in the doorway, she added, "As far as I know, Stephan is safe and sound and—if I'm any judge—very happy."

"As far as you know?" He walked into the room to stand before her, his eyebrows rising steeply. "What's that supposed to mean?"

"It means that he was all that and more the last time I saw him."

"And when was that?"

"Three weeks ago when he left to go on his honeymoon," she said casually.

"His . . ." Dan closed his eyes and counted to ten, then said calmly, "Sit down, Arlie, and tell me all about it."

She sat on the couch and smiled up at him warmly. "Now I know I'm really home. Nobody has counted in my face for three years."

He chuckled suddenly and sat down beside her, his arm along the back of the couch. He turned to look at her. "Don't try to tell me no óne has lost his temper with you in all that time."

"Oh, plenty have lost their tempers. They just never bothered to control them. Not many people have your restraint." She took his large hand and squeezed it tightly. "Oh, Dan, I'm so glad to be back."

"Don't try to sidetrack me, Arlie. What's going on?"

Arlie sighed and dropped his hand. "It's very simple. Stephan and I are . . . divorced and he has remarried."

"When did all this happen?" Dan said, his voice not quite shocked, but definitely surprised and holding an indefinable element. "You didn't say anything about it in your last letter."

"It happened kind of suddenly," she explained. "He met Connie and knew immediately that she was the person he wanted." Arlie looked up at Dan, an enthusiastic expression on her face. "They're so right together, Dan. You can tell when you look at them. I like her very much. And I really think she'll make Stephan happy."

He studied her expression with deep intensity,

his glance probing hers sharply. "You don't exactly sound like the rejected wife."

"Of course not," Arlie said cheerfully. "I love Stephan and want him to be happy. And Connie is what he wants."

"If you love him so much why did I read at least once a month about your love affairs—with everyone in Europe? Everyone except your beloved husband."

"You know how they exaggerate that stuff," Arlie scoffed. "Stephan and I both have had a lot of fun, but we didn't let it spoil our relationship."

"Fun! You call sleeping with every man on the continent fun?" he asked, his tone of voice conveying his feelings of disgust even more forcefully than his words had.

"Well . . ." she hesitated as though considering the question, then grinned when he glared at her. "I'm teasing. I didn't sleep—"

"No, I'm sure you didn't do much *sleeping!* And to be fair I know that the first affair was Stephan's, but that doesn't excuse your actions." He rose in agitation, running a hand through his hair, and began to pace. "I can't understand it, Arlie. You were never promiscuous." He stopped to look at her, his voice growing softer. "No one knows better than I that you were sensual, even as a teenager. You enjoyed being touched." He closed his eyes and said gruffly, "Enjoyed hell! You reveled in it." He opened his eyes, but avoided looking at her as he continued to pace. "But you were never promiscuous," he repeated. "What happened to you? Were you so disillusioned with Stephan that you felt you had to retaliate? You never said a word about it in your letters. But every time I picked up a newspaper or magazine, there you were. You and your lovers. Your name has become synonymous with free living and free loving. Everyone knows of the notorious Arlie Fleming, but what happened to Arlie Hunicutt? The little girl who couldn't stand wearing shoes and was so honest it hurt."

Arlie leaned her head back against the couch, closing her eyes wearily. She hadn't expected this from Dan. Dan was her stability, her core. She answered his accusations quietly. "I still hate wearing shoes and I'm as honest as I know how to be." She opened her eyes to look up at him. "I've never denied those rumors because I didn't think I had to with you. Most of what you read came from the overactive imaginations of some scandal sheet journalists. Some of it was based on fact—I admit that. Does it change your mind about me? Am I no longer worthy of your friendship?" She stood and walked to her shoes, looking down as she slipped into them. "I wouldn't want to contaminate the purity of your mind, Dan. So I'll find somewhere else to stay."

"Arlie, wait," he said as she began to walk out of the room. He caught up with her and turned her around to pull her into his arms. "I'm sorry, little bit," he murmured against her dark hair. Arlie shivered as he used the name he had always called her when she was hurt or scared. "I've given you a lousy welcome home, haven't I? Of course it doesn't change things between us. Nothing could. You know that."

Arlie felt emotion building inside her. Emotion she was too tired, too confused to handle. She needed to put their relationship back on its normal footing. She sniffed delicately, tears welling up in her dark blue eyes on cue, and said in a tremulous voice, "I thought you hated me, Dan. It was aw . . . ful." She sniffed again and looked up at him with huge, pathetic eyes. Dan stared into her eyes, suspicion slowly replacing the concern in his. Then his lip started to twitch uncontrollably.

"You monster," he laughed. "By God, you almost fooled me. After all the times I've seen you pull that trick, you'd think I'd know better."

Stepping away from him, Arlie slid out of her shoes again and smiled smugly. "I had you for a minute. I must be better than I thought." She walked back to the couch to sit down. She knew she would have to talk to Dan about the reputation she had gained in the last three years, but now was not the time. She would have to let him in on the facts gradually.

When he joined her on the couch, she turned to him and asked, her voice serious, "Is it all right if I stay with you for a while? I know it seems that I've taken it for granted, turning up with all my luggage like this, but I can make other arrangements if it's not convenient."

"Don't be stupid," he said, his voice irritated. "Forget what I said a minute ago. None of that is my business. I was just worried about you."

"I know," she murmured. "I do want you to know about all that. How things happened and why they happened, but that can wait until later. I'm glad it's okay for me to stay, because I lied about making other arrangements." She looked at him with an unconcerned smile. "The truth is I'm stone broke."

"How could you be broke?" he asked, his brows rising in astonishment.

"Well . . . you know the arrangements Daddy made in his will? I was supposed to get a quarter of the principal when I married, then I had to live on the interest until I reached thirty, at which time I would inherit the remainder." Dan nodded and she continued. 'The money that I got when Stephan and I married ran out about a year ago. We used it to set up his practice and . . . well, on having a good time. Since then we've been living on Stephan's income—which is not enormous—and the interest. But when Stephan and Connie married I wanted them to have a really nice wedding and honeymoon, plus extra money to carry them through until Stephan's practice is better established." Arlie looked down at her hands and began to carefully examine her fingernails. "So I borrowed six months' worth of interest from the estate."

"You did what?" he bellowed, his eyes blazing.

"Don't yell at me. I arranged with Daddy's attorneys to get an advance. The problem is they won't let me have another penny for at least five months." She looked up at him, a beatific expression on her face. "I've got forty-two dollars and thirty-nine cents in my purse and no visible means of support. Can I stay here until I find a job?"

"And what in the hell do you think you're going to do?" he fumed. "You're crazy, do you know that? Do you honestly think you can go out and find a job, in a twinkle of an eye? You've had no kind of training at all . . . unless you're thinking of becoming a *fille de joie*. I don't understand this hold Stephan has over you. Ever since you met him you can see no one else. You give him everything he wants and then worry that it's not enough." He looked down at her, his brown eyes flashing angry fire. "You wasted one quarter of your inheritance on him—not to mention three years of your life—and now you've left yourself penniless so that he can be comfortable. What kind of a man would accept that sort of sacrifice?"

"He didn't know, Dan," Arlie explained urgently. "He didn't know that I was borrowing money for him. I always handled our finances. So he had no idea we were so low on money." She looked away for a moment. "I know you've never liked Stephan.

You thought he was surly and rude and after my money. But you don't know what his life was like before I met him. He changed after we married. He learned to look outward instead of being so introspective."

"Oh, he looked outward all right. At every woman who passed by," Dan said contemptuously.

"I don't want to talk about Stephan," Arlie said firmly. "We'll never agree about him. I simply want you to know that I won't be sponging off you while I'm here. I'm going to get a job and save up enough money to get my own place. Wait," she said as he started to interrupt. "I know I haven't trained for anything, but I can find something. I don't care what it is. I'll wash dishes or wait on tables and go to school at night. I need something to do. I'm twenty-six. Old age is waiting just around the corner and I can do nothing of value."

"Oh, I don't know about that," Dan said, grinning reluctantly. "There has to be an opening somewhere for a feisty little broad who can ski, play tennis, ride like a jockey, surf, and dance until all hours of the morning. And I'm leaving out your most celebrated area of expertise. That alone should get you more offers than you can handle."

"Very funny. I'm serious, Dan. And I wish you would cut out all the comments about my love life. You'll give me such a complex, I won't be able to kiss a man without wondering if I'm living up to my reputation," she said ruefully. "Speaking of love life, I like Diane. Is it serious?" Arlie mentally crossed her fingers. Her future plans depended on Dan's answer. She really did like Diane and wouldn't do anything that might possibly hurt her.

Dan hesitated before answering. "I thought for a while it could be, but we seem to have drifted into a nice, easy friendship. I think she's found someone else who interests her." Before she could determine Dan's true feelings his look suddenly became sharper. "What's with you and Eric?"

"I've only just met the man, for heaven's sake. He asked me to have dinner with him tomorrow and I accepted." She grinned audaciously. "You have very nice friends. I like him, too."

"I'll just bet you do," he muttered. "You seem to be moving awfully fast. I'm not going to warn you about him—in fact, I should probably warn him about you—but I hope you know what you're doing. And for God's sake don't pull any of your stunts while you're with Eric. The Prescotts are friends as well as business associates. Diane's father owns a monthly news magazine and I've done a lot of political stuff for him. I don't want any tension in our relationship."

" 'Oh, ye of little faith,' " she said, pouting. "Do you really think I would do anything outrageous? No, don't answer that," she said before he could answer. "Trust me. I won't go skinny dipping in hotel fountains or lead poor Eric astray in any way. I promise I'll keep him away from the seamy side of my life."

"You're an idiot!" He laughed, giving her a quick hug. "I'm not worried about Eric, but Mr. and Mrs. Prescott are another proposition. They're very conservative and your name alone may be enough to cause a stir."

"Would you rather I didn't go out with him?" Arlie asked, her voice losing its playful lilt.

Dan avoided her eyes and hesitated before answering, "No, of course not. I wouldn't keep you from enjoying yourself."

After a moment of thought Arlie decided not to question his answer. If he had doubts about her seeing Eric he would tell her in his own time.

"You said you had done some work for Diane's father? I'd like to see it. It seems as though every time I've picked up a magazine in the last couple of years I've seen one of your cartoons. I'm so proud of you. You've come a long way in such a short time." She chuckled softly. "I don't see how you've kept out of jail. You've stepped on some pretty important toes. Your caricature of that fat senator was hilarious, not to mention libelous." Dan's satirical cartoons had grown steadily in popularity over the years and were now quoted as often as the stock market index.

Dan laughed, relaxing once again. "He didn't think it was very funny. That bilious bastard tried to sue me. Until my attorney presented him with a few well-documented facts." He stretched his large frame and looked down at her. "You're probably exhausted. I'll show you your room. Would you like something to eat first?" When Arlie shook her head emphatically he continued. "Then I'll go out and get the rest of your luggage while you are freshening up."

"That sounds lovely." Arlie sighed in contentment. "I've been dreaming for hours of a hot bath and I'm afraid the time difference is catching up with me."

He stood and pulled her to her feet. "You have a nice sleep and tomorrow we'll worry about a suitable occupation for you."

He showed her upstairs to a large, airy, pale green bedroom. The comfortable looking bed in the center of the room seemed to pull Arlie toward it, but she resisted it bravely as Dan showed her the adjoining bath. After putting her suitcase on the bed he started to leave the room, then stopped and turned back to look at her. "I guess I forgot in all the excitement, but—welcome home, Arlie." He stared at her face for a few seconds, then wheeled and quickly left the room.

Dearest Daniel. He was her best friend, her confidant, her advisor. Anything she had learned about being a responsible human being she had learned from Dan. He had begun guiding her at their first meeting. And when he discovered Arlie had been emotionally abandoned by her father and left in the care of servants who, though decent people, had little time for molding the character of a volatile little heathen, he had taken on the responsibility himself.

Which probably explained why he was so upset with her, she realized as she removed her robe from the large suitcase Dan had left on the bed. It had to be like a parent seeing all his careful teaching being ignored by a thoughtless child.

Arlie sighed deeply as she thought of the intricate tangle her life had become. Tomorrow, she promised herself. Tomorrow she would tell him the whole story and once again ask for his help.

She walked into the adjoining bathroom, chuckling suddenly when she saw the sparkling white fixtures. Dan considered colored fixtures in the bath and kitchen decadent. She filled the large tub with steaming hot water, grinning wickedly as she added pink foaming bath oil, then stepped in to soak the weariness from her body.

When she found herself nodding off for the third time Arlie decided it was time to leave the soporific warmth of the tub and find a more conventional place to sleep. She dried her body quickly and slipped into the blue silk wrap, knotting it loosely at the waist.

In the bedroom the drapes had been drawn against the still-bright early afternoon sun. Through the cool shadows she saw the remaining pieces of her luggage sitting at the foot of the bed. Dan must have brought them in while she was in the bath. She considered unpacking to get it out of the way, but decided that since her clothes had waited this long, a few more hours in an over-stuffed suitcase wouldn't hurt them.

The cover on the large bed had been turned back to expose crisp, white percale sheets—another sign of Dan's Spartan background—and Arlie shrugged out of her robe eagerly. As she lay the silk wrap across the end of the bed and sat down, a gleam of silver on the bedside table caught her eye. She looked closer and her mouth suddenly tilted in a warm smile of remembrance.

Lemon drops. He had brought her lemon drops just as he had on their first meeting. She could see him now as he had been when she was six years old. He had looked down at her from what had seemed like an enormous height, his unruly red hair flaming in the sun. Arlie had stood there, fearless despite her sudden capture, and looked him over with eyes eons older than should have reposed in her six-year-old head.

At fourteen he had seemed all arms and legs. Lean and lanky with large, awkward looking hands. But it hadn't been his gangly limbs that had held her interest. It had been his face. And it was his face that had gained Arlie's reluctant trust. White teeth behind firm, mobile lips. The shallow cleft in his angular chin. His emphatic nose with the bony bump on the ridge. And bushy red eyebrows that brought attention to his deep-set, striking brown eyes.

She had examined his face slowly at first, star-ing with haughty bravado, then with a bewildered feeling that was close to pain. In her belligerent six-year-old mind she hadn't known that she was feeling the loss of warmth, of love, when she looked at Dan. Because she had never come in contact

with those emotions, she didn't recognize on a
conscious level the hurt and the yearning she felt
inside. She only knew that she could trust this
boy who looked like a man to her young eyes.

He had taken her into his care then. Laughing
at her wisecracking view of her small world, scold-
ing her when she misbehaved. Always teaching.
Always guiding her, throughout her turbulent
growing years. Arlie's father, the big fish in their
small central Texas pond, was a snob, pure and
simple. When he had discovered her friendship
with Dan, he had violently opposed the association,
forbidding her to see him again.

But by this time Arlie was older and stronger
and she defied him continually until he resolved
the problem by ignoring it. Her father could never
understand why Dan's friendship was so important to Arlie. And he couldn't understand why all
the teenage girls in their small community wanted
more than friendship from such an awkward,
homely young man. But Arlie knew. Arlie had
seen Dan's smile.

In her early teens, all her late night fantasies
had centered around Dan. Elaborate dreams in
which Dan on a white charger had rescued her
from a changing cast of evil villains. Or dreams of
Dan declaring before the world that he loved the
girl whom everyone described as a hellcat.

Then when Arlie was seventeen her puppy love
had suddenly turned into a violent, secret passion.
Secret because Dan at twenty-five still saw her as
his charge, his special burden. That is, he did
until the warm June night she made her feelings
known.

Arlie shivered suddenly as she thought of that
night. It was odd how she always avoided thinking of it and of the events that followed. It was as
though she and Dan had made a secret, unspo-

ken pact to wipe the memory away. They had never referred to it again. Until today. Dan had been so busy chastising her—as he always had when she did something wrong or thoughtless—that he had slipped up and mentioned what happened that night in the gazebo.

Arlie pulled the sheet that smelled of sunshine up over her head, an old habit that always reappeared when she was confused and needed to think. She knew she was probably cutting off the oxygen to her brain, but she didn't care. It was a comforting habit.

Maybe it was time for her to take the memory out and examine it, find out why she had always avoided thinking of it. It had been Dan's twenty-sixth birthday and Arlie had spent the day searching through all the stores in Fort Worth for the perfect gift. She had found it in a small, shabby looking jewelry store on the south side of the city. It was a long gold chain carrying a beautifully sculptured golden bird. An albatross. The awkward goony bird that Dan always compared her to. Now she would truly be the albatross around his neck.

She had called his apartment, barely able to keep the excitement out of her voice, and asked him to meet her in the gazebo at ten o'clock. A tryst in the moonlight had appealed to her young, dramatic nature. She had spent hours agonizing over what to wear and how to arrange her waist length hair. The dress she eventually chose was pink and soft and sophisticated, making the most of her immature curves. She had pulled her hair back into a loose knot on the nape of her neck, hoping that she looked like Audrey Hepburn.

At ten she peeked out the window to make sure Dan was there before her. She had her entrance all planned. She would stand bathed in moonlight, and Dan would be so mesmerized by her ethereal beauty that he would declare his love on the spot. At least that was the plan, but somewhere in the events of the night her plans went sadly awry.

She had appeared in the archway of the gazebo, the moonlight illuminating her figure just as she had planned, giving an unearthly silvery glow to her lovely features, and Dan had said, "Well, it's about time. Now what was so urgent that I had to hide out here like a secret agent in one of those junky movies you go to all the time?"

Arlie sighed. Things were definitely not going according to plan. He didn't seem in the least mesmerized by her loveliness. "I brought you a birthday present," she said softly and moved into the shadows of the summer house.

"That's sweet of you, brat. But couldn't you have given it to me in the daylight so that I could see what it is?" His voice was indulgently amused, but there was also an underlying hint of wariness.

"It's not that dark. Look at the moon. Isn't it beautiful, Dan? Why does it have that strange blue cast to it?"

"I don't know, Arlie." His voice was suddenly stiff as she moved toward him in the shadows. "You'll have to look it up in the encyclopedia."

"Oh, you always say that." She sighed.

"It's the best way to learn," he said turning away from her, his voice tight.

Arlie moved to stand behind him. "There are some things that you can't learn from an encyclopedia, Dan," she whispered huskily.

Jerking around suddenly to face her, Dan said harshly, "What in hell are you up to, Arlie? I don't know what game you're playing, but you can cut it out."

She looked down at his clenched fists. "It's not a game," she said quietly. "I only wanted to give you your birthday present." She looked up to see the skepticism in his face. "Okay, maybe that wasn't all. Maybe I wanted you to see me as an adult just once. I'm not a kid anymore, Dan. I'm eighteen and I'm all grown up. I wanted to give you the birthday present as an adult . . ." She looked down at the floor. ". . . and maybe give you a birthday kiss, also as an adult. Is there anything wrong with that?"

He was silent for a moment, then he sighed and tilted her head so that he could see her face. "Of course there's nothing wrong with that, little bit. I'm sorry I blew it all out of proportion. It's just that I thought . . . well, never mind what I thought." He put his arms around her and pulled her close. "I would be honored to receive your first adult kiss, Miss Hunicutt."

Arlie grinned suddenly, shedding her artificial sophistication as she tiptoed to reach his lips. He bent his head and their lips met in a soft, friendly kiss. Then suddenly a new element entered the kiss. Arlie didn't know whether she or Dan was responsible for the change, but her lips parted of their own volition and the kiss deepened. Their bodies were unexplainably closer, Dan's hard, wiry strength pressing into her budding softness.

Twice during the next magical minutes, Dan tried to pull back with a gruffly spoken curse. But the look of sensual longing on Arlie's face brought him back to her lips each time and moments later they were lying side by side on the padded chaise longue.

His hands seemed to have a will of their own as they sought her small, high breasts beneath the silk dress. Arlie was so involved in the unfamiliar sensations pulsing through her body, that she almost didn't see the look on Dan's face. He was in the grip of some fierce emotion that recognized neither time nor place.

He began to slide the tiny strap from her shoulder and ease the soft fabric down over her swelling breast, his breathing becoming harsh and raspy, when he stopped, a stunned expression freezing his craggy features.

"Daniel?" she whispered huskily, then shivered as he slid from the chaise and stood with his back to her. His shoulders were stiff and tense, almost as though he were angry, then he shuddered heavily and ran his fingers through his hair before turning to face her.

"Go in the house, Arlie." His voice was stern and strangely cold.

"But, Dan . . ." she began to protest, straightening her dress as she stood to walk toward him.

"I said go in the house," he repeated harshly.

Dan's anger had finally penetrated Arlie's confusion and she had left him there in the moonlight, her heart throbbing painfully. If only she could shed some of the hurt through tears. But tears never came to Arlie when she was hurt. She could call them up easily enough when she was playing a prank, but somehow, when the pain spread through her body, tightening her muscles, threatening to burst in her chest, the tears refused to come and release the anguish.

So she had sat dry eyed in her darkened room that night, hiding behind the curtain, and had watched him leave the vine-covered gazebo. She had remembered then with a choking laugh that he hadn't opened the gift she had brought for him. She wondered if he had even bothered to take it, but the next morning when she crossed the dew-sprinkled lawn after a long and sleepless night the small beribboned package was missing.

Arlie didn't hear from Dan for two weeks after

his birthday and she didn't seek him out. When they did meet by accident the air between them was charged with tension. Arlie had felt confused and embarrassed by his obvious rejection and Dan had seemed preoccupied and distant.

For days Arlie struggled with doubts. Doubts about her relationship with Dan. Doubts about her worth as a human being. Beneath her outgoing personality lay an ego that was all too easily bruised. Dan's rejection seemed to reaffirm all her old insecurities. Then after a lengthy bout with self-pity, Arlie came to some surprisingly adult conclusions. Dan was meant to be a friend. A friend she loved dearly, but nothing more. If he had wanted to deepen their relationship, he would have made a move on his own without her machinations. When she had thrown herself at him, he had reacted instinctively, as any man would, but he had stopped it before it went too far because he simply didn't care for her in that way. But that didn't diminish the strength of their friendship. It only put it in the proper perspective.

With the death of her childish dreams had come a new maturity. Arlie finally made the decision to go to Dan and try to reestablish their old friendship. Then one day as she walked through the woods behind her house, wondering how to approach him, he had suddenly appeared. As he stood on the path in front of her, the sunlight streaming through the branches of the trees turned his hair into a flaming beacon. She stood still, her eyes wary and watchful, the sight of him filling her with an indescribable sense of loss.

He had looked down at her face for interminably long, silent moments, then smiled his crooked smile and murmured, "Hello, brat."

Arlie had flown down the path, flinging herself into Dan's waiting arms. As he held her tightly, she had known that everything would be all right. As long as she had his friendship, she had no worries for the future.

But, of course, she hadn't known then about Stephan. Under her percale tent, Arlie shivered suddenly as she remembered the arguments, the near-break in her friendship with Dan that followed her introduction to Stephan. Dan's acceptance of her relationship with a man he had considered unstable had been slow, but the strength of their friendship had carried them through once again.

And on the day Arlie had left her familiar world behind to begin her new life with Stephan, Dan had been there to see them off. He had stood in the airport lounge, looking grave as he examined the jealousy in Stephan's eyes, but throwing nonstop instructions at Arlie. She was to write regularly. She was to keep out of trouble—if she could. She was to take care of herself.

And so she had left him, emotionally secure once more. Of his list of instructions, writing regularly was the only one she had managed to follow. And tomorrow, one way or another, she would have to find a way to tell him that shelter was not the only thing she needed from him.

Tomorrow, she told herself firmly. Then she reached out to touch the small dish of lemon drops, her eyelids drooping wearily. Maybe it could wait a few more days. After all, there was no rush. And with the contented sigh of a confirmed procrastinator she closed her eyes and surrendered to sleep.

Three

"Arlie! Arlie Fleming!"

Arlie looked over Eric's shoulder toward the sound. She searched the small, crowded dance floor for a moment, finally shrugging when she saw no one who looked familiar. The small, exclusive country club that Eric had chosen for their dinner date was filled to overflowing with young, laughing couples. Their dinner had been excellent, as was the music from the trio on the tiny stage and Arlie was enjoying herself immensely, luxuriating in the blessed anonymity she was finding in this crowd of strangers.

She had slept away most of the day, awakening to find a note from Dan on her nightstand saying he wouldn't be in until late. She had used the time to explore his domain, rifling through his closets and kitchen as if she had the right. On finding preliminary sketches for a cartoon strip in his studio, Arlie had been unreasonably annoyed that Dan was absent when she wanted so much to share her enthusiasm with him.

She would have to remember to ask him about it tomorrow, she resolved silently, looking over her shoulder when she again heard her name being called. She was turning back to Eric's questioning look when she saw a horribly familiar face across the room, its owner eagerly pushing his way through the gyrating couples.

"Oh, no," she moaned, turning back to Eric with a hunted look in her eyes.

"Who is it?" Eric asked, craning his neck to find the cause of her panic.

"Wolf," she muttered in frustration. "Can we leave now, Eric? Before he gets here."

"Wolf? What kind of name is Wolf?"

"It suits him, believe me," Arlie said. "His mother wanted to be a concert violinist, but she married instead, very dramatically giving up her career for love and a dog food fortune—for which the music lovers of the world thank her. When their first child was born she quite naturally named him after her hero." Arlie turned and indicated the large, gaudily dressed man who was steadily drawing closer. "So there you have Wolfgang Amadeus Schwartz."

"You're kidding," Eric choked out through his laughter.

"No, I'm not. And he's closing in on us," she said urgently. "Come on!" She grabbed Eric's arm and began to pull him toward the exit. But her efforts were in vain. Before they had taken three steps, Arlie felt a hand on her shoulder halting her escape.

"Arlie, pet. I can't believe it. Why didn't you tell me you were coming to Texas?" Although Wolf's voice was not high, it had the ear piercing quality of fingernails on a blackboard, so that anyone who was acquainted with him automatically and unconsciously assumed a pained look on seeing his approach.

"Hello, Wolf." Arlie sighed in resignation, turning to face the puffing, red-faced man. "It all happened so fast I didn't even have time to get in touch with my *friends*." The implied insult went completely over his head and Arlie continued. "And of course you were in South Africa when Stephan got married. I left immediately afterward."

"I hear that was some party you threw for Stevie and his little nurse." His pudgy fingers grasped her forearm, directing her with not-so-subtle tugs toward a table on the edge of the dance floor, and as he spoke his eyes were glued on the expanse of creamy flesh above her strapless dress.

Arlie stubbornly dug in her heels and refused to move another inch. "Connie is an excellent anesthesiologist. And in case you hadn't noticed, I'm not alone, Wolfgang." She indicated Eric, smiling maliciously when she saw the obese man's lips tighten at her use of his proper name. "This is Eric Prescott. Eric, this is Wolf Schwartz of the dog food Schwartzes." She watched as the two men acknowledged her introduction, Wolf eyeing the handsome, younger man warily, Eric responding with a look of awe on his face, his blue eyes twinkling with fun.

"*The* Wolf Schwartz?" Eric said enthusiastically. "I must tell Mumsie. She wouldn't buy anything but Schwartz products. I believe you also make a scented kitty litter that's marvelously innovative."

Wolf's eyes were narrowed in suspicion. "I wouldn't know," he said stiffly. "I don't keep up with the boring details." He turned to smirk at Arlie. "I only spend the checks. Right, pet? And now that you are rid of your precious Stevie, you can help me." He glanced at Eric. "I'm sure you won't mind if Arlie goes with me. We have to talk over old times. Do you remember Kiki Zolner's party last summer?" He ran one finger over Arlie's bare arm, causing her to shiver in disgust. "Arlie here has been the hottest thing on the continent for the last three years. Some of us even considered reviving the art of dueling to do away with the competition."

"It's certainly a thought," Eric muttered, staring at the plump fingers on Arlie's arm. "I'm afraid you'll have to reminisce another time. Arlie and I are expected at the mayor's house in," he glanced at his watch, "fifteen minutes. Her presence was specifically requested and it would be an outright insult if we didn't show up." As he talked Eric maneuvered her away from the grasping hands. "It's been thrilling meeting you, Mr. Schmaltz. We'll have to get together real soon." This last was said over his shoulder as they walked away.

As Eric's Peugeot pulled out of the country club parking lot, Arlie turned to him and said, "Schmaltz?" The laughter bubbled up inside her, overflowing in an infectiously musical sound. "Kitty litter?" she gasped. "I knew I was going to like you the minute I set eyes on you, Eric."

"Ditto, I'm sure," he replied demurely, laughing with her. "Is that overweight subhuman really a friend of yours?"

Arlie shuddered. "How can you even ask? Stephan and he had some pretty wild times together, but I always managed to avoid prolonged exposure to his 'charm.' For some reason he reacts to me like Pavlov's dogs to a bell and starts to salivate every time I appear."

"For *some* reason? Don't you know that you're gorgeous?"

"Gorgeous?" she asked, grinning. "Not gorgeous. Terribly attractive maybe. Or even hauntingly lovely. But not gorgeous."

"I stand corrected. But whatever you call it, it certainly causes a man's blood pressure to soar."

"Are you sure it's not my reputation rather than my looks that causes men to react the way they do?" she asked quietly. "I had hoped to get away from all that, but as soon as I saw Wolf I knew my past wasn't going to die gracefully."

"I hate to disillusion you," Eric said, "but even if Schwartz weren't around to tell everyone what hot stuff you are, you still couldn't escape your reputation. Fort Worth may not be New York or Paris, but we read the scandal sheets just like the rest of the world. We even have jet setters of our own who bring us all the latest gossip."

"I realize that, but I thought I would be in a different crowd with Dan's friends." She sighed. "Last time I saw him, his friends were less influential people. Nice, ordinary people who wouldn't know Arlie Fleming from Harpo Marx."

"And it bothers you that people know all about you?"

"Yes," she said emphatically. "I'm more than ready to leave life in the fast lane. I want people to know and like me for what I am, not what they think I am. I'm tired of that look I get when I meet someone new. If it's a woman, she starts to wonder why someone as ordinary as me should be considered a femme fatale. If it's a man, he's wondering if I'm as good in bed as he's heard." She turned to catch Eric's speculative glance. "You see. It's in your eyes right now. You're thinking, 'Well, are you?'"

"You're right," he admitted. "I'm sorry if that offends you. But honestly, I'm not going to try and rush you into anything, Arlie. I'll admit I'm salivating just like our obnoxious friend at the country club, but that's not the only reason I want to be with you. When I looked into your eyes at Dan's house yesterday, it was like looking in a mirror. Do you know what I mean?"

"Yes, I do. I felt it, too."

"I gather from what Schwartz said you've recently divorced and your ex has just remarried, so maybe things are simply happening too fast for you."

"Maybe," she said doubtfully.

"We'll just take it easy and let things happen naturally." He pulled the car over to the side of the road. "I don't repulse you physically or anything like that?"

"No, of course not." Arlie laughed. "And thanks for not pretending that you weren't thinking what I knew you were thinking. I admire honesty and I would be very glad to have you for a friend until I get a few things straightened out in my head." Among other things, she thought ruefully.

He leaned over and gave her a brief, soft kiss. "Friends . . . temporarily," he murmured. "Now, how would you like to go for a moonlight sail?"

"A sail? I thought I was going to get to meet the mayor," she said, her lower lip drooping in a pout. When he grinned appreciatively she said, smiling, "I'd love to go for a sail. Do you have a boat?"

"Yes. Which is a good thing because it's very difficult to sail without one," he said as he pulled the car back on to the road.

Minutes later, they entered Dan's house and Arlie left Eric in the hall and ran upstairs to change. When she returned, taking the steps three at a time in her enthusiasm, she found Dan standing where she had left Eric minutes earlier and her blond escort was nowhere in sight.

"Where's Eric?" she asked, peering over Dan's shoulder to try and see into the living room.

"What in hell are you wearing?" he asked, squinting at her outfit as though dazzled by it. "It makes me dizzy to look at it."

Arlie looked down at her bright orange jeans and the splashes of orange, pink, and purple in her sweatshirt. "I'll have you know this was designed especially for me by a very talented new English designer. Percy said it was a 'visual expression' of my 'effervescence and *joie de vivre*.' He said it was *me*."

"He could be right. You always make me dizzy, too."

Arlie grinned, then sobered suddenly as she remembered why she had changed clothes. "What have you done to my beau? We were going for a moonlight sail."

"So he said," Dan replied casually. "But he decided to go home instead."

"*He* decided?" Arlie asked suspiciously. "Or you decided? Why didn't he stay to say goodnight? What did you say to him to make him leave?"

"I told him you were a carrier of a newly discovered social disease," he said in an evil whisper. "I said it doesn't affect you, but anyone who makes love to you will find all the hair on his chest falling out. His gold chains will turn green, then he'll find himself irresistibly drawn to polyester leisure suits. He couldn't get out of here quick enough," Dan finished airily.

Arlie tried very hard to look stern, but failed miserably. Her lip twitched uncontrollably and she began laughing at the picture he painted. "You're terrible. What did you really tell him?"

Dan put his arm around her and walked her toward the stairs. "I told him that you are starting a whole new life and you need time to adjust before becoming involved with someone else." He stopped her indignant protest with a finger on her lips. "I also told him that your new life includes a job and you need to be up bright and early tomorrow to find one."

She considered his statement for a moment. "You're right about the job. But you still had no business interfering, Dan." Her eyes sparkled as she smiled in anticipation and said, "I'll get you for that one. And you should know better than anyone that I never forgive and forget."

Dan's eyes narrowed as though remembering her mischief of the past. "Arlie, you little . . ."

"Dan?" The soft, feminine voice came from the direction of the living room.

Arlie turned toward the sound, her eyes gleaming. "Why, is that Diane?" she asked sweetly. "Why didn't you tell me she was here? I simply *must* go and say hello to her."

"Arlie," he began, trying to block her way.

She ducked under his outspread arm with the agility of a cat and walked into the living room, quickly adjusting her features to give her face a look of heartbreaking poignancy. "Diane," she sighed as though it were an effort to speak. "I didn't know you were here." She darted a fearful look at Dan. "Maybe I shouldn't have come in."

"Don't be silly," Diane reassured her, giving Dan a puzzled look. "Of course you should. You promised to finish that naughty story you were telling me yesterday."

"I don't think I'd better tell you any more about my past." Arlie's lip quivered suddenly. "Dan doesn't want me to annoy his friends."

"Annoy?" Diane turned to Dan, whose face was becoming an alarming shade of red. "What is she talking about, Dan?"

"Arlie . . ." he said, gritting his teeth, his voice low and threatening.

"Don't let it bother you, Diane," Arlie said with quiet dignity. "I'm used to it." She gave a broken laugh. "Dan's afraid I might corrupt his friends. Especially your brother." She blinked her eyes several times to keep the tears from overflowing and swallowed audibly before turning her shimmering, sad eyes to Diane. "I guess I won't be seeing you again. I'll probably spend most of my time in the bedroom."

She turned away, bravely squaring her shoulders, and began to walk out of the room. As she passed Dan, she looked at his tightly clenched fists and winked audaciously, grinning irrepressibly when she heard his choked curse. She ran gaily up the stairs, whistling softly under her breath, then smothered a wicked chuckle when she heard Diane's, "Daniel Webster, what on earth have you been doing to Arlie?"

Arlie stretched, her hands behind her neck lifting her loosened hair, her back arching as she stood on tiptoe. The blanket and sheet on her bed were turned back neatly and she had already changed into her short, wispy silk nightgown, but she wasn't sleepy. Walking to the nightstand, she popped a lemon drop into her mouth, wondering which of the books she had bought in London would put her to sleep most quickly.

Suddenly she remembered the raspberry sherbet she had seen in Dan's freezer. That would be perfect. She would placate her sweet tooth, read a murder mystery, and forget about sleep.

The decision made, she swung down the stairs to the kitchen. Dan was still gone. She had heard him leave to take Diane home over an hour ago. He hadn't had a chance yet to castigate her for her performance in the living room, but she knew it was coming. He would bellow at her and she would apologize, then they would laugh.

Thirty minutes later Arlie sat cross-legged in the center of the bed, the bowl of bright pink sherbet forgotten in her lap, the mesmerizing novel open before her. She was so absorbed in the intriguing mystery that she didn't hear her bedroom door open and was completely oblivious to Dan's presence until a shadow fell across her book. Startled, she jerked her head up, steadying the partially melted mass in her lap as it threatened to overturn.

"Dan!" she gasped. "You scared me. You should never sneak up on a person who has just witnessed a decapitation."

"Hello, Arlie."

Dan's voice was quiet and casual, but his eyes told a different story. The moment of reckoning was at hand and Arlie eyed him warily as she straightened her legs and slid to the opposite side of the bed. "Now, Dan," she began as he walked slowly around the end of the bed toward her.

"Do you remember how I used to handle one of your little escapades?" he asked, his voice soft and dangerous.

"I'm too old to spank," she said, clutching the bowl to her chest as though it would protect her from his revenge.

"You think so?"

As he shortened the distance between them, Arlie panicked and set the bowl on the nightstand, picking up the spoon which held the last remaining lump of semi-solid sherbet. She held the spoon up, tipping the bowl back with one finger, ready to catapult the soggy mass. "Take one more step, mister, and you're dead where you stand," she threatened.

"You wouldn't," Dan said, hesitating momentarily.

"Oh, wouldn't I?" She grinned, enjoying her power. "Just take another step and we'll . . . oh, Lord!" The liquid had caused her finger to slip from the spoon and Arlie closed her eyes tightly, refusing to see if her unintentional assault had hit the target.

The room was suddenly still and quiet, not one word coming from Dan, and finally Arlie could stand the suspense no longer. She slowly opened her eyes to find her worst fears confirmed. Rivulets of pink liquid were turning Dan's face into a neon road map.

"Oh, Dan," she whispered, biting her lip to hold back the laughter. "I'm sorry. I didn't mean to—I swear." Moving forward as he extended his tongue to catch a trail of pink on his lip, she lifted the hem of her full but short gown and began to mop ineffectually at the mess.

"That's enough, Arlie," he muttered as she smeared it across his cheek. "I'll do it myself. Why on earth I put up with you, I'll never . . ."

Suddenly he stopped speaking and it was a few seconds before Arlie felt a strange tension in the silence. Dan's breathing had changed oddly and he held his body stiff. She glanced away from the pink spot on his chin to look into his eyes. "Dan?"

But Dan wasn't listening. His eyes were trained on her body. Lifting the side of her gown to wipe his face had pulled the thin apricot silk tight against her frame, molding it to her curves, outlining her firm, rounded breasts and slender hips.

"Dan?" she asked again as he continued to stare.

He glanced up at last, his brown eyes vague and distracted. "What?" he murmured, then caught the puzzled look in her eyes and turned away, running his long fingers nervously through his unruly hair. Without another word he walked to the door to leave.

"Dan," she said again, bewildered by his strange behavior.

He stopped as he reached the door, turning slightly toward her, not looking at her, but at least acknowledging her presence.

"I'm sorry if I embarrassed you in front of Diane. Please don't be angry with me," she murmured. "If it will help, I'll call her and apologize."

"Don't bother," he muttered brusquely. "If you want to play silly games that's your business," then he turned again and walked out, unaware of the hurt in Arlie's eyes.

As soon as he closed the door behind him, she sat abruptly on the bed, dazed. Dan had never acted like this before. He had been angry and exasperated and even disappointed in her, but he had never acted so coldly toward her, as though what she did no longer mattered to him.

Then Arlie remembered. He *had* acted this way before. This was exactly the way he had acted after she had met him in the gazebo on the night of his twenty-sixth birthday. Vague and distracted and . . . indifferent. Either her behavior tonight— and she admitted she had acted like a witless juvenile—had brought out the same reaction in him or there was something else bothering him. Something that had nothing to do with her.

Diane. He had been gone so long when he took Diane home. What had he said about her? He had thought things were serious between them, but Diane had found someone else and now they were just friends. Maybe Dan wanted more than friendship from Diane. Maybe he was hurting. Maybe the blonde woman meant more to him than he would admit.

Arlie jumped up from the bed. If Dan was

hurting, then Arlie had to try to help him. He had always been there when she needed help, so it was only fair that she return his care. Opening the door, she glanced toward his darkened bedroom. Then the clinking sound of glass drew her attention to the living room and she walked down the stairs, her bare feet treading silently on the thick carpet.

She walked to the living room door and saw Dan across the room, his back to her as he raised a glass to his lips and swallowed the contents in one gulp. In the mirror above the sideboard she saw his face and hastily stifled a gasp of distress. There was such anguish, almost fear, in his face, that Arlie felt her heart leap to her throat. She pressed back against the wall outside the door and knew she couldn't let him see her. Dan would hate being observed at such a moment. The emotions he was feeling were deep and private and, friend or no friend, Arlie had no right to intrude.

She turned and walked quietly back up the stairs. After bathing and donning a clean gown, Arlie turned out the overhead light, leaving only the bedside lamp for illumination, and lay down on the bed. She picked up the discarded murder mystery and began to read, but her attention kept wandering back to the muffled sounds of Dan's movement.

He was restlessly prowling the room below. The movement was so familiar, Arlie could see him clearly in her mind's eye. This was the way Dan always tackled an unsolvable problem. He was a man of action and when no action was possible it frustrated him unbearably, resulting in the restless pacing.

But as she heard the repeated chink of glass on glass Arlie knew that something new had been added to his familiar habit. He had not drunk heavily three years ago. Wine with dinner and an occasional beer had been his limit. She had no idea whether this addition had been acquired along with his expensive house and growing fame or was simply a result of some inner stress he wasn't willing or ready to share with her.

She sat up abruptly as Liszt's *Hungarian Rhapsody* blared in through her closed door. She smiled wryly, reclining again as he turned the volume down to a more conventional level. The frantically happy music was not exactly the lament for a lost love Arlie would have chosen in Dan's mood, but then she should have expected this kind of perversity from him. He diligently avoided anything that resembled mawkish sentiment.

The despair she had seen in his face haunted her and Arlie resolved to do something about it as soon as possible. Without Dan's knowledge, of course. She simply couldn't stand the thought of his being unhappy. If he liked small, blonde women, then, by God, she would find him a whole house full of them. They wouldn't be Diane, but they would certainly take his mind off her for a while, because they would adore him. How could they not? Arlie couldn't understand how someone as intelligent as Diane could let something as precious as Dan's love slide through her fingers.

Arlie jerked upright suddenly as she heard a loud crash from the living room. She swung her feet to the floor and began to walk toward the door in concern, then stopped and chuckled softly as she heard Dan apologizing to a chair. He's really tying one on tonight, she thought and moved back to the bed to lie down again with a helpless sigh.

After his encounter with the chair, the sounds

from below faded to intermittent, muffled thumps and Arlie slipped gradually into sleep. She was dreaming peacefully of her childhood when something penetrated her slumber. It was not a sound that shook her from her unconscious state. It was the intense, piercing sensation of being watched. She jerked her eyes open, coming instantly awake, and moved her head warily to the large, shadowy figure at the end of her bed.

"Daniel," she sighed in relief. "You idiot, you scared me out of ten years' growth." She reached over to turn on the bedside lamp, but hesitated as she watched him move around the end of the bed to stand beside her. "Is something wrong?"

"No," came the nonchalant, almost breezy reply. "Everything's just . . . fine. Perfectly fine." He was articulating his words in a peculiar, stilted fashion as though he were taking great care with each syllable.

She could see him more clearly now. He was dressed for bed, his broad, furry chest bare, the pants of his pajamas riding low on his lean hips. Arlie tried to read his expression, but his face was obscured by the enveloping darkness and she reached again for the lamp, only to have her hand grasped firmly.

"Arlie?"

"Yes?" She answered softly, confused by his strange mood.

"We're friends, aren't we?" His voice sounded amused and almost sly as though he were enjoying a private joke.

"Of course we are. That's a stupid thing to ask. What on earth are you—"

"And friends should give comfort and succor. Don't you . . . think so?"

"Yes," she said doubtfully. Where was he leading?

"Arlie, I need comfort and succor tonight." She felt rather than saw his smile. "You're a very generous woman. Be generous to me. Succor me." He smiled again, savoring the sound of the word.

"Oh, Dan," she said, rising to her knees. "I know you're troubled and I swear I'll do anything I can to help." She reached out to touch his face with her free hand. "Would you like to talk about it?"

He gave a gruff, choked-off laugh. "You always were a little dense." He pressed her hand to his chest. "Talking wasn't . . . exactly what I had in mind. I was thinking of something a little more . . . physical."

My God, she thought in astonishment. He must be bombed out of his mind. Dan would never have suggested anything like this if he were sober. Apparently the alcohol hadn't dulled his need for Diane and he was trying to find another brand of oblivion. Arlie knew without a doubt that he would regret his suggestion tomorrow when he was again hitting on all cylinders. Now it was up to her to subtly ease the idea out of his mind before the situation went beyond the point where he could forgive himself.

"Darling," she said gently. "I don't think that would be a good idea. You're not yourself tonight. You have . . . things on your mind. If you feel the same tomorrow, then of course that would put a whole different light on the matter." Arlie smiled indulgently, pleased with the reasonable way she was handling the situation. "Now, why don't you go on to bed and . . . ooooh!" With astonishingly agile movements for such a large man, he flipped her back onto the bed and was now lying on top of her.

"You talk too much," he muttered against her neck.

"Dan," she said tightly, trying to regain the wind that had been knocked from her lungs when his weight had landed on her. "Dan . . . get off!" She pushed at his chest, but it was no use. He had the strength of ten men. So much for subtlety. She maneuvered her knee against his thigh, but he shoved it back in the careless, unconcerned manner of a man shooing a fly.

"You smell wonderful," he whispered, moving his lips down her neck to her delicate breastbone.

"And you smell like a brewery," she said between clenched teeth. "You big ape, get off of me . . . now!" Suddenly, she stopped struggling. This strategy was definitely not working. He was strong enough to subdue her most frantic efforts. She would have to outthink him, which should be no difficult task considering his condition.

"Oh!" she said, widening her eyes ingeniously. "What was that?"

"Mmmm?" he murmured, lowering his lips to the rounded tops of her breasts.

"I heard a noise downstairs," she said urgently, wiggling a hand free to clutch his shoulder.

He lifted his head and slowly raised his eyes from her smooth skin. "What? I didn't hear anything." He had relaxed his guard on his speech and the words were slurred and drawling.

"I'm sure I heard something."

Raising himself up on one elbow, he turned his head to the side as though listening for the elusive sound. It was the opening Arlie had been waiting for. Catching him offguard, she shifted her body in a swift sideways movement and scrambled off the bed, but she had only managed to take one step before she felt him catch the flowing material of her gown and give it a hearty yank. As she sat abruptly and unwillingly, his arms came around her from behind.

"Gotcha," he said, chuckling.

"This is not a game, you overgrown fool," she muttered in exasperation. She raised her hand to nibble with great concentration on one manicured nail as he began to nibble with great concentration on the side of her neck. In all the years she had associated with people who changed their sex partners almost as often as they changed their clothes, Arlie had not run across a man she couldn't handle. If a man had not attracted her, she had always managed to let him know diplomatically and without too much damage to his ego. But using diplomacy on the big lump behind her would be like trying to reason with an eggplant. Even sober, Dan had the tenacity of a bulldog when he got an idea in his head. Inebriated, he was hopeless.

Arlie shrugged involuntarily as Dan began an assault on the sensitive nape of her neck. She leaned her head forward in a moment of weakness and he raised one hand to brush aside her silken fall of ebony hair, holding her fast with the other. The soft caress of his firm lips on her vulnerable skin sent delicious, shivery sensations rippling down her spine and she sighed in uncontrollable pleasure. Then suddenly Arlie realized what was happening to her and she raised her head abruptly, the back of her skull connecting sharply with his.

"Hellfire, Arlie," he growled, releasing her to rub the top of his head. "That hurt."

He looked so indignant, so much himself, that Arlie couldn't stop herself from laughing. And that, she found, was a very big mistake. He stared at her laughing face, his eyes bemused, as though mesmerized by the sound of her laughter. Then he reached out and before she could even comprehend the magnitude of her mistake in not taking advantage of her sudden freedom, she found herself once more beneath him, his body pressing hers into the soft bed.

Groaning in exasperation, she tensed her muscles, preparing to renew her efforts. Then Dan's soft, pleading whisper reached her ears. "Let me love you, Arlie." The husky sound touched a hidden chord and she was lost, relaxing her body under his hard frame, allowing his strength into her softness, accepting his touch for the first time since he entered her bedroom. After all, her sensual self whispered insidiously to her reluctant brain, this is what you came for, isn't it? Take it now and worry about the explanations later.

"Yes," he moaned, feeling her compliance, unknowingly echoing the persuasion of Arlie's sensual side.

He lowered his head slowly and when his lips were almost touching hers, she raised her head the last fraction of an inch to meet him eagerly. The sweetness of the kiss filled her, drugging her, pulling long-repressed memories to the surface.

She was carried away by a dream that had begun for her in her turbulent youth and begged for completion now. She yielded breathlessly as he deepened the kiss, his tongue searching the sweet recesses of her mouth, his large hand finding her breast and caressing the taut nipple through the silk of her gown. Spreading her legs with his knee, he fitted his length intimately to hers, his throbbing warmth sending urgent messages to her body.

He raised her hands to his chest. "Touch me," he said in a thick, raspy whisper.

Arlie needed no second bidding and he groaned in satisfaction as her fingers spread in the thick fur of his chest, finding the heated flesh beneath, kneading the muscles, learning the texture of his body. Sight was an inadequate sense compared to the depth of what she was learning with her touch. She slid her hands over his shoulders, exploring each rippling muscle, each tendon, each bone. She was hypnotized by the feel of him. She smoothed ardent fingers up to his strong neck and encountered a chain, its delicacy surprising her. The fine strand of gold didn't fit what she knew of Dan. She slid her hand down the length of the chain, suspicion dawning, and found what she was seeking. It was the golden albatross.

Arlie caught her breath sharply. The gift she had given him so many years ago. The gift he had accepted while rejecting her. She lay perfectly still, sanity catching up with her at last. She couldn't do this to Dan. Last time he had felt ashamed of his reaction to her advances. He had let lust momentarily cloud his judgment—just as lust and alcohol and his feelings for another woman had taken away his reason tonight. Arlie owed Dan the chance to make a decision with a clear mind. She couldn't take advantage of his weakened condition knowing he would hate himself when reason returned. Sighing deeply, she slid from beneath him and got to her knees, beginning to move to the side of the bed, but was halted by a hand on her hip.

"Arlie, damn it," he muttered. "What are you doing now? You are the most perv . . . the most verp . . ." He seemed to be having trouble making his lips form the word. "You are the most cock-eyed female I've ever met," he amended finally.

She sympathetically patted the hand that lay on her hip and said, "I know, love. And I'm sorry but I've changed my mind."

"You can't," he stated firmly, rising unsteadily to his knees. "It's not allowed. I wrote the . . . rules and last minute withdrawals are not . . . allowed."

"Now, Dan, don't get difficult," she said sternly, turning to face him on her knees. "We'll talk about this tomorrow when you're sob . . . not so tired."

"I'm not tired," he denied. "I'm fresh as a dai . . . fresh as a . . . I'm fine."

"You're fresh, all right," she muttered under her breath and began to inch away. But now both his hands were on her hips and he held her fast. "I'm giving you one more chance to let me go, Dan," she warned. Then as she heard his deep chuckle, she shifted sideways, drew back her fist and connected swiftly with his chin in a solid, meaty thunk. Blinking in astonishment, she watched as his eyes opened wide in surprise, then he seemed to drift in slow motion back down to the pillow.

"Oh, Lord," she gasped, scrambling toward him. "Dan?" She touched his face, muttering, "Well, why in hell didn't you tell me you had a glass jaw?" She turned his face toward her and suddenly he smiled peacefully, mumbling unintelligible words, and snuggled his head into the pillow.

He was asleep! The bumbling idiot was actually asleep. She sat back, glancing at him with a disgruntled look on her face. Now what was she going to do? There was no way she could get him back to his own bed. She would just have to leave him here and sleep in his bed. He would feel like hell in the morning when he remembered how he got in her bed, but there was nothing she could do about that. At least he would wake up alone and not have to wonder if he had violated their friendship. She could spare him that anyway.

Suddenly Arlie looked again at his sleeping form, a new thought growing in her mind. Why should she spare him anything? Didn't he deserve a little torture as repayment for tonight? A devilish light appeared in her eyes, a wicked grin turning up her lips as she flopped down beside him and cheerfully pulled the covers up over them both.

Four

Arlie turned her head, trying to get away from the tickling sensation under her nose. For a moment she was five years old and Herman had once again decided to sleep on her neck. Then she remembered. Dan, she thought, smiling. Very carefully she opened her eyes. He was still sleeping peacefully, lying on his side, his long arm thrown carelessly across her neck. Stifling a chuckle, she hurriedly closed her eyes as he turned on his back and began to rouse.

She could feel him come slowly awake, then as realization dawned he became still and tense. She heard his muffled, groaning "Oh, God," and allowed herself to raise her eyelids in bewilderment. She looked into his wary brown eyes, deep disappointment growing in her face and evident in her whispered accusation. "Oh, Dan. How could you?"

she asked. Turning away from him, she buried her face in the pillow.

"Arlie," he began hesitantly, apologetically.

She shook her head violently, rejecting any explanation, any excuse. "How could you abuse our friendship like that?" she said, her voice breaking slightly. "I trusted you and you took my trust and smashed it . . . *smashed it* with your disgusting animal lust." Arlie was rolling now. She pounded her fist into the pillow, jerking away from his hand on her shoulder, her long hair flaring out to cover her face. "I came to you for help and you used me basely." She moaned. "You've satiated your slathering appetites, Dan, but you've destroyed my faith in humanity . . . forever." Turning over on her back in agitation, she threw an arm across her face and peeked at him from beneath her forearm.

He was lying back on the pillow, his eyes closed, his face slack with relief. "Nothing happened, did it?" he asked quietly.

"Nope," she admitted cheerfully, pulling herself up to wrap her arms around her knees.

He turned his head to look at her, his eyes narrowed to slits of sable fire. "Why didn't it?"

"I slugged you," she said, smiling sweetly as she rested her head on her knees, her face turned toward him. "Actually, I think it was due more to your booze than my brawn, but you went out like a light."

"I don't know," he muttered, reaching up to rub his stubble-covered jaw. "You always did have a mean left hook." He sighed, closing his eyes briefly, then said, "I'm sorry about last night. I should have my ass kicked for trying something like that." He looked away, avoiding her eyes, his voice a little distant. "I'm sorry I took my personal problems out on you."

"Why?" she asked reasonably. "I've been doing it to you for years. If felt nice being on the other end for once." She hesitated, chewing on her lip. "Dan," she said finally, "Is it your relationship with Diane that's bothering you? Would you like me to talk to her?"

"No!" he bellowed, raising himself on one elbow, then sinking back to the pillow with a groan of pain.

"That's what you get for yelling," Arlie said with self-righteous satisfaction. She reached out to touch his forehead. "Poor Dan. Does it hurt? Maybe it was something you drank."

Opening one bloodshot eye, he looked her over as though she were a particularly repulsive species of bug that had just crawled out from under his private rock. The fire kindling in his eyes had her tensing her body for the blast she knew was coming, but before he could cut loose the doorbell rang, and Arlie sighed in relief. "Someone's at the door," she announced happily—and unnecessarily. "Would you like me to get it since you're . . . uh . . . indisposed?"

"No," he muttered emphatically. "I'll get it." He rose slowly and painfully from the bed, touching his temples gingerly as the doorbell sounded again. When he reached her bedroom door he turned back to look at her. "I'm going to overlook the fact that you chose to stay in here last night instead of sleeping in my bed. I figure I deserved the scare I got when I woke up. But . . ." His eyes sharpened. ". . . don't think I don't realize that my reaction was exactly what you had in mind."

"But, Dan . . ." she protested in a small voice, fluttering her absurdly long lashes at him.

"Oh, shut up," he grumbled as he left the room to the sound of her laughter.

Arlie bounced from the bed, humming as she

pulled on her robe, her mind filled with possibilities for the future. Dreams for herself and dreams for Dan, even though he would be horrified at the thought of her plotting to help him through his emotional crisis. She was headed for the bathroom to change when the voices coming from the entry hall struck a familiar welcome chord. Pulling open the door that Dan had left ajar, she stood for a moment at the head of the stairs, listening. Then with a gasp of delight she hurled herself down the stairs and threw herself into the arms of the man who stood just inside the front door.

"Stephan," she breathed, laughing her pleasure. "What are you doing here? Why didn't you let me know you were coming? Where's Connie?" She shot off the questions in rapid-fire succession, her deep blue eyes glinting with excitement.

"Slow down," the husky, dark-haired man said, chuckling at her enthusiasm. "Last question first. Connie is right here." He turned, gesturing toward Dan, who had evidently found time to pull on a white terry cloth robe.

Arlie leaned around to see the tall, thin woman with short, brown curls who had been hidden by Dan's width. "Connie!" she squealed, moving to embrace the smiling woman. "What happened to the honeymoon? It was supposed to last another two weeks. And why are you here in Texas? What—"

"Arlie." Dan's voice, quiet and firm, broke into her questions. "Why don't we go into the living room and sit down. Then if you'll keep quiet long enough to let either of them speak, I'm sure they'll be glad to explain."

Arlie laughed in apology. "I've been babbling, haven't I? Dan's right. Come in, both of you, and sit down." Linking her arms through Stephan's and Connie's, she urged them into the living room.

Stephan stared at Dan for a moment after they were seated, a grudging respect showing in his eyes. "How did you do that?" he asked, smiling quizzically. "If I had asked Arlie, politely or otherwise, to shut up, she would have told me to shove it."

"Stephan!" Arlie protested. "That's a fib. I wouldn't have been so rude."

"Okay, so you wouldn't have been rude. You would have smiled, patted my arm, and then done exactly what you wanted to do. You are the most pig-headed—"

"That's enough, Steve," Connie said firmly, coming to Arlie's aid. "Arlie wouldn't listen to you because ninety percent of the time you were busy screwing up your own life. It hurt your credibility just a tad, love." She smiled up at him, her eyes shining with love for her new husband.

Smiling ruefully, Stephan acknowledged her statement with a mumbled, "I guess so," and acknowledged, too, the look in her eyes with a gentle squeeze of his hand.

Arlie watched the loving byplay between the couple on the couch and emotion welled up inside her, tightening her chest. For the thousandth time, she blessed this woman who had made Stephan whole and blessed also the instinct that had sent her to Connie with the facts. Facts that Stephan refused to give her. Facts that made it possible for Connie to accept Stephan's love and return it freely.

She glanced up and caught Dan's piercing eyes trained on her from across the room. He moved from his position at the fireplace to the leather chair next to her, his gaze never leaving her face. Shifting uncomfortably at the suspicion in his sharp brown eyes, she turned back to Connie and

Stephan and said, "I've stopped babbling." She raised her arched eyebrows expectantly.

"So you have," Stephan said. "I don't know where to start. We were lying on the beach in Jamaica, talking about our plans for the future and suddenly it seemed stupid to wait. We knew our honeymoon wouldn't end with Jamaica so we decided to bring it to Texas with us."

"Wait for what? What plans and why Texas? I thought you were going to keep your practice in Paris." Arlie bit her lip, forcing herself to stop the barrage of questions. But the vague information he had given her had only stimulated her curiosity.

"Let me explain," Connie said, laughing. "It's hard for us to keep our feet on the ground, Arlie. But I'll try to make more sense than Steve." She paused a moment as though remembering. "We did a lot of talking in Jamaica. Real talking. After hearing about Stephan's . . ." She glanced warily at Dan. ". . . background. We both decided it was still too much with him and he would never really be free of it until he went back and faced all the old ghosts that still haunt him. In the beginning, we had only planned a short trip to Curry."

Arlie's eyes locked with Stephan's as Connie mentioned their hometown. She looked for anger or hurt or maybe even fear in his eyes, but he smiled reassuringly and she returned her attention to Connie.

"As we talked about the trip something began to grow in Stephan. Or maybe resurface is a better word. Stephan began to remember things about Curry that didn't include pain. The more we talked, the more enthusiastic he became about the visit. The whole thing came to a head when he called a friend who still lives in Curry. Adam Morgan."

Arlie jerked her eyes back to Stephan's in shock. "A friend? Your old probation officer?"

Stephan nodded. "He was a friend, Arlie. I didn't know it at the time, but he was." He turned to look at Dan. "You know Adam, don't you?" At Dan's nod, he continued. "Do you know what he's planning?"

"The clinic?" Dan asked, his eyes reflective. "Yes, we've discussed it. I think it's admirable, but to tell you the truth, I'm afraid he's taking on more than he can handle."

"Clinic?" Arlie asked, looking from Dan to Stephan. "What kind of clinic?"

"Adam has spent his life helping troubled boys," Stephan explained. "Kids who have nowhere else to turn. Kids in the same situation I was in when I first met him. Now he wants to expand that. Instead of helping them in his spare time, he wants to establish a place that's recognized officially. A place that's open around the clock. A place staffed with qualified people who can handle any situation that arises, be it legal or emotional. Things as simple as finding them a place to stay for the night or as difficult as keeping them out of jail."

"It sounds wonderful," Arlie said. "But what does it have to do with you?"

Connie took up the explanation again. "After Stephan spoke with Adam, it was like a fire had been lit in his brain. He ached to be in on the project. And who is better qualified? He doesn't have to imagine what these kids are going through, he knows. He's been there." She smiled up at Stephan. "So it didn't take much encouragement for him to call Adam back and offer his help."

"You'll be living in Curry?" Arlie asked, excitement and doubt warring within her. "But your practice was going so well. This venture doesn't sound very . . . lucrative. Will that be a problem?"

Seeing the doubt in Arlie's face, Stephan laughed

a little wryly as though he were mocking himself. "Don't worry, Arlie. We'll be fine. The project has some federal funding. The rest will come from private contributions. My salary will be minimal, but we've faced that and it's just not that much of a drawback. Connie will have her work and we're prepared to live simply." He smiled. "More than prepared. We'll welcome the change."

"Connie?" Arlie looked to the woman beside Stephan for an echo of Stephan's conviction.

"My first husband was wealthy, Arlie," Connie said quietly. "So I've been poor and I've been rich. But what you don't seem to realize is that *then* I was poor. Now I'm rich."

For an unbelievable moment, tears shimmered in Stephan's eyes as he looked at his wife, then he cleared his throat roughly and shifted his gaze to Arlie. "So you see, my darling protector, we really are going to be just fine."

"Yes," Arlie confirmed huskily. "I think you are."

Before the emotion-filled silence could grow unwieldy, Dan broke in, asking questions about the couple's honeymoon, Connie's work, and Stephan's thoughts on the success of the clinic. In the beginning when he addressed his questions to Stephan, Dan's voice was stiff and polite, but slowly he began to relax and show a genuine interest in the younger man's opinion. This seemed to surprise Dan as much as it did Arlie, for occasionally he would pause in the middle of an absorbing discussion, his eyes narrowing momentarily as he looked at Stephan, then he would give his head an almost imperceptible shake and continue.

Later as the two men began another intense debate, this time on politics and Dan's cartoons, Arlie slipped away with Connie to make breakfast. In the kitchen she closed the door, then turned to

Connie and said, "He really is going to be all right, isn't he?" It was more an expression of wonder than a question.

"Yes," Connie replied simply. "Thanks to you."

"Me?" Arlie said in astonishment. "No, not me. I couldn't give him anything." She closed her eyes briefly. "As hard as I tried, I couldn't give him what he needed."

"Arlie, think for a minute. What would have happened if he hadn't met you? He went through law school on a scholarship, thanks to Adam Morgan. But he was ready to use his knowledge to fight the law. He was still rebellious and headed down a path that could only lead to prison . . . or worse. You took him away from that. You gave him all the things he had dreamed about. Money, influence, entrance into the charmed circle. But more important, you loved him. For the first time in his life someone looked beneath his rough exterior and found something to love." Connie leaned against the gleaming white counter and laughed weakly. "You can't imagine how jealous I was the first time he told me about how you had loved him and made him open up to you. There was a deep, shining gratitude in his eyes. No, more than that. Arlie, he worshipped you for what you gave him."

"But in the end it wasn't enough," Arlie said quietly. She grinned suddenly. "If you wanna talk jealousy, you should have seen me when I realized you were the one who was going to wake him up and make him whole. He began to grow the very day he met you."

Connie came to Arlie and gave her a quick hug. "The only thing I gave Stephan that you couldn't was the ability to give to me. He is as necessary to me as the air I breathe. You love him, but he doesn't keep you alive." Connie paused, shivering suddenly, then shook her head briskly and continued. "We could sit here all day applauding each other for what we've done for Stephan, but the truth is he would have reached this point on his own, without the help of either of us. It would have taken him a lot longer and it would have been infinitely more painful, but he would have eventually reached the same end."

Arlie was thoughtfully silent for a moment, then she said slowly, "Yes, I guess you're right. He would have. He's a man now, Connie. I know it shouldn't amaze me, but it does. I keep wanting to say, 'My, my, how you've grown,' like a doting aunt."

Connie laughed gently at Arlie's observation and, suddenly, like a magnified echo, they heard masculine laughter from the living room. Recalling their reason for being in the kitchen, they hurried to prepare breakfast.

Dan and Stephan's political discussion carried them through the leisurely breakfast and would very likely have carried them through lunch as well if Connie hadn't intervened, reminding Stephan of their appointment with Adam.

At the front door as Connie questioned Dan about the housing possibilities in Curry, Stephan drew Arlie aside and said quietly, "How are things going? You said you were going to get a job. Have you found anything yet?"

"I haven't really had a chance to look, but I'm not worried. Something will turn up that's exactly right for me." She clasped his hand. "And don't you worry either. I'll be fine."

"I know. Sometimes I feel like I deserted you, then I remember how strong you are. And, oddly enough, I resent it. I wish there was something I could give you that you really need." His eyes were strangely wistful as he looked down at her.

"You know what you gave me, Stephan. It was

something I had always dreamed of and never thought to find. Only you could have given it to me," she said earnestly.

"It was that important to you?" he asked, wanting to believe her.

"Oh, yes," she confirmed, smiling. "It was that important."

With Stephan's arm circling her shoulder, she turned to say good-bye to Connie, but found her eyes held by the change in Dan's face. The relaxed, friendly look had vanished and in its place was a sharply determined, almost hostile, expression. She murmured her good-byes reluctantly, hoping to escape to her room as soon as the smiling couple left, but as the door closed behind them she knew it was useless to run. Dan stood there, looking at her with a dark intensity.

"I think I'll go get dressed," she murmured hopefully.

"Yes," he said after a moment. "You do that. And then I want to see you in the living room. The curtain goes down today, Arlie." His voice tightened as he spoke. "If I have to use a thumbscrew to get you to talk, one way or the other, you're going to tell me what in the hell that charade was all about."

Five

Arlie felt Dan's eyes on her back all the way up the stairs. She wished she had stuck to her original plan and told him the whole story as soon as possible. She could then have spared him the confusion of her reunion with Stephan and Connie. But, well, how on earth could she have anticipated them turning up out of the blue like this?

She shrugged, pulling the bedroom door closed behind her. Hindsight was less than useless now. She would just have to make the explanation as simple and clear as possible. Moving quickly, she pulled on bright yellow shorts and a matching striped T-shirt, ran the brush through her hair, anchoring it high with a covered rubberband, then turned to leave the room, anxious now to get the explanation over with. Dan had been in the dark long enough.

When she reached the living room, however, she found she would have to wait a little longer, for the room was empty. She began to pace in agitation, then stopped abruptly, chuckling as she realized she was copying Dan's habit of wearing out the floor when action wasn't possible.

"I'm glad you think it's so funny."

Whirling around, she saw Dan standing behind her, a frown darkening his features. He had changed his clothes and was now wearing faded black Levi's and a white cotton shirt, the sleeves rolled up to just below the elbows, the neck open loosely, allowing her a glimpse of a thin gold chain. A smile of pleasure spread across her full lips as she thought of how it had hung around his neck all these years.

"Maybe you'd like to share the joke, Arlie?"

Irritation was building in his voice and Arlie hurried to correct his mistaken impression. "Now don't get testy," she said soothingly. "I was laughing because I found myself pacing like you always do. I was all set to explain everything and you weren't here." She walked to the couch to sit down, curling her bare feet up beside her, and patted the cushion next to her. "Come sit down, grumpy, and let me play Scheherazade."

The tension dropped from his face as he sat beside her, curiosity forcing him to put aside his role of heavy father. "What kind of holy mess have you gotten yourself into this time, pest? That was the weirdest thing I've ever witnessed in my life." He shook his head in disbelief. "I knew you still loved Stephan so I was prepared for that . . . but your reaction to Connie threw me completely. You acted as though she were a vision at Lourdes. How can you—still loving Stephan—treat her like your long-lost buddy, with not one hint of jealousy?"

"Oh, there was jealousy—or maybe envy is a

better word—in the beginning, but if you only
knew what she's done, you'd understand."

"So tell me."

Arlie hesitated for a moment to gather her
thoughts, then began slowly. "I'll have to go back
to the beginning, Dan . . . for you to understand
everything. So be patient, okay?" At his impatient nod, she smiled and continued. "It began
the summer I was ten. Do you remember the time
you found me hiding under the porch of the old
Wilkins' house?"

Dan didn't have to search his memory. He responded immediately. "Of course I do. You were
scared to death when I hauled you out from under
that crumbling old place." He raised his hand to
stroke her cheek absently, caught up in the past.
"And you wouldn't let me help you. For the first
time, you wouldn't tell me what was bothering
you."

"I was ashamed," she explained quietly. "I was
so mixed up . . . and afraid. Afraid you would stop
caring if I told you the truth."

"Arlie!" he said, his voice shocked. "How could
you think . . ."

"Oh, I know," she said, interrupting his ex-
clamation. "*Now* I know that it wouldn't have
made any difference, but at that time I couldn't
take a chance." She pressed her face against his
hand. "Let me explain. Daddy and I had had another of our arguments. Only this one was worse
than usual." She sighed. "I can't really blame him
for the way he reacted to me. He was so conservative, so conscious of his position in the
community, and I was so wild. We were bound to
clash. I don't even remember what started this
particular argument . . . some prank of mine that
he considered disgraceful and it probably was . . .
but I certainly remember how it ended. He was

screaming at me—I had never seen him so mad—
then he said he should have expected that kind of
behavior from me, knowing who had fathered me.
He said it was bad enough that he had lost my
mother, but why did he have to be reminded of
that bastard every time he looked at me." Arlie
closed her eyes briefly, seeing but not really taking in Dan's stunned expression. "I was so dumb.
He had to practically spell it out for me before I
finally understood what he was saying."

"God, Arlie," he breathed harshly, pulling her
into his arms to hold her tightly. "Why didn't you
tell me? You were too young to handle something
like that alone." He curved his long fingers around
the side of her face, lifting her head so he could
look into her eyes. "Why didn't you let me share it
with you, little bit?" he asked gently, his eyes
dark and compassionate.

"Like I said, I wasn't too bright back then." She
laughed shortly, mocking herself. "I figured there
was something there that made it impossible for
Daddy to love me. I couldn't take a chance on you
reacting in the same way. So I kept quiet. It was
years before I found out who my real father was
and that there was nothing shameful about the
way I was conceived."

"How did you find out?"

"When I was old enough, I simply went to the
courthouse and started to look through their
records. I found a marriage certificate that proved
my mother and real father had married three years
before I was born. I looked through the divorce
records and found nothing so I went on to the
death certificates. Seven months before I was born,
John Randall was killed in a job-related accident."
She paused for a moment. "I had to go through old
newspapers to find out any more about him. Then
I knew why Daddy despised him so much. He was

a driller on an oil rig. Just an ordinary man . . . or maybe common is the word Daddy would have used."

"I'm sorry, Arlie," he said softly.

"Don't be," she said rubbing her face against his shoulder in an affectionate feline gesture. "It's not a present pain. And even then I think I was a little relieved. It explained so much . . . why Daddy didn't love me. Why he was unable to accept my love. And why he seemed to resent the simple fact that I *was*." She grinned suddenly. "Up until then I just thought I was repulsive."

"Idiot," he said, smiling in return, but his eyes sharing her old hurt. "I'm glad you finally told me, but what does all this have to do with Stephan?"

"Nothing . . . everything . . . it may help explain our relationship better. I was nineteen before I found out all the facts about my birth. I had been through all the records at the courthouse and the library, but so much was still missing. How did my mother come to marry a man like Daddy? And why would a man who was so painfully class conscious marry a woman who was pregnant with a laborer's child? So knowing I could never approach him for the answers, I started sneaking into Daddy's study and looking through his personal papers, hoping to find a clue. Eventually I found what I was after in a drawer of old letters. Daddy was so orderly . . . he never threw anything away." She sighed deeply, shifting her position slightly. "It was sad really. He loved her before she married John Randall. And when my real father died, Daddy used Mother's pregnancy as an excuse for them to marry right away. They left town so that no one would know that I wasn't Daddy's child. I suppose if she had lived he might even have come to accept me," she added wryly. "Anyway, while I was searching for information about my background,

I found something else. Something that turned out to be much more important than a tragic old love."

"Yes?" he prompted as she hesitated.

"The first letter I found didn't mean anything to me. It was a fairly recent letter from a woman demanding money for her son. As I said I really didn't pay much attention to the first letter, but I kept coming across them. The same type of letter, always from the same woman, always demanding money for her son. The dates on the letters spanned quite a few years and by the time I found the original letter, I was definitely intrigued, but I still hadn't put two and two together. It was quite a shock when I found a letter, from the same woman, telling Daddy he was going to be a father. I couldn't connect that kind of affair with someone like Daddy."

Dan whistled softly through his teeth in amazement. "Do you mean that stiff-necked old scoundrel had an illegitimate son? And he kept all the evidence where anyone could find it?"

"I think the drawer being unlocked was an accident. It looked as though someone had gone through the contents recently. I suppose he had been looking for something and simply forgot to lock it afterward, because the next time I tried to open it, it was locked."

"And his son? Do you know who he was?"

"Luckily I had copied the woman's address that first time. I didn't do anything for several weeks, but I couldn't get it out of my mind. I tried to picture what he looked like. What he was doing. What his reaction would be to me. I was becoming obsessed with a boy I had never even seen, a boy whose existence I hadn't even dreamed of before then. Finally I drove by the house where he was supposed to live, never consciously intending to stop, but it seemed impossible to get that close and not stop. So I did."

"Why?" he asked. "I mean, I can understand you were curious, but is that the only reason?"

Arlie rose from the couch and walked to the fireplace, feeling his eyes on her. She was coming to the most difficult part and she wasn't sure how Dan was going to react. "You know it wasn't," she said, sighing heavily. "You know how much I had always wanted a brother or sister. I used to watch you with Susie and Mike and wish you were my brother instead. There were times that I almost hated them because they had you and didn't even know how special that was."

"You had me, too," he quietly reminded her. "I know it wasn't the same as a real brother, but this boy wasn't a real brother either. Why was it so important to find him?"

"Don't you see," she said, walking to stand before him. "If Daddy hadn't told me that he was not my father, this boy would have been my brother. Oh, I know he wouldn't really have been. But I would have thought he was and that's what counts."

Dan pulled her back to her former position beside him. "Cockeyed reasoning, but I see what you mean. So, how did the reunion go? Did he know about you? Was he as anxious to have an almost-sister as you were a brother?"

"He wasn't there. The woman—his mother—said she didn't know where I could find him. I think she knew who I was. It's very likely, considering the size of Curry. She seemed to find it amusing that I was looking for him." Arlie shuddered, remembering the greed in the woman's small, sly eyes. She had known then that the boy she was looking for had had a much worse life than she'd had and she felt more determined than ever to find him.

"Anyway," she continued, "after a little detective work, I found him. He was quite a surprise. I hadn't done any calculations on the dates of the letters and had expected to find a boy, maybe a young teenager, but I found instead a man four years older than me." She grinned suddenly. "And we definitely did not have a joyous reunion. He knew who I was, but more important, he knew who he was. I think, at first, he hated me. I had all the things he had wanted, still wanted. All the things he felt he was entitled to. So it was a little hairy in the beginning. He was so wild and he was determined to shock me. All those years I thought I had a reputation for wildness in Curry, but to him I was still a proper little rich girl and, being a genuine junior hoodlum, he tried his best to scare the socks off me. Of course," she glanced at Dan, mischief dancing in her eyes, "he didn't know about my tenacity then."

Dan frowned in confusion. "Why didn't you tell me all this at the time? Where was I when all this was happening?"

"I tried to tell you, but you wouldn't listen."

"You never tried to . . ." he began vehemently, then paused, his eyes widening as though struck by a sudden thought. "When, Arlie? Precisely when did you meet him?"

She glanced down at her hands in her lap. "August of the year I turned nineteen."

"Stephan?" Dan breathed in astonishment, not needing her relieved nod for confirmation. "Of course it was Stephan. That's why you were so entangled emotionally from the very beginning." He took a deep breath. "So you went looking for a brother and found a lover instead."

"Actually . . . no," she said slowly. "In the beginning he was too full of resentment to listen to anything I had to say. He let me hang around because he got a kick out of trying to shock me. When I finally convinced him that he couldn't get rid of me, that I cared, he was so pleased . . . no, that's too mild to describe the effect it had on him. Even though he tried not to show me, it really meant something that I—a real Hunicutt— was willing to recognize him as my brother. If I had told him about my background it would have negated the whole effect."

"When did you tell him the truth?"

"The truth is, I never did get around to telling him that I'm not really his sister." She spoke slowly, gazing carefully into space while she waited for his reaction. It was several minutes before he finally broke the tense silence.

"You mean he married you thinking you were his sister?" Dan's voice was peculiarly uneven as though he didn't know whether to be shocked or not. "Is he some kind of nut?"

"No, Dan," she hurried to reassure him, laughing unsteadily as she realized what he was thinking. "It wasn't like that at all. It was that damned will. I don't know what I expected, but I never thought Daddy would leave me all his money. If I had given it any thought at all I would have known that Daddy wouldn't do anything that would cause speculation in town. The same reason he never recognized Stephan as his son." She shook her head regretfully, feeling sorry for the man who had let public opinion rule his life and rob him of so much. "If he hadn't left me his money it would have caused quite a stir and he just couldn't face that. So he had to leave all his money to someone he couldn't stand."

You don't know that, Arlie," Dan said softly. "Maybe he came to his senses at last."

"You don't really believe that," she said, smiling sadly. "We both know what he was like." She shook her head, leaving the old sorrow behind. "When the will was read, it seemed so wrong. I wasn't his daughter. He didn't even like me and he left me all that money. I didn't want the blasted money and I had no real claim to it, while the rightful heir wanted it desperately. I couldn't just hand it over to him because of the terms of the will. The only way I could get my hands on it was to marry."

She looked at the flame kindling in Dan's eyes. "And don't ask me why I didn't come to you," she said irritably. "I did try to talk to you about it, but every time I mentioned Stephan you jumped down my throat. You really were unfair to him, Dan. You were so righteous in your condemnation of his behavior. You refused to see that there was more to him than his surface roughness."

Dan sighed, his eyes showing his regret. "I know. I should have listened to you. But to tell you the truth, I was scared. You always listened to me before you met him, but I could see you becoming more and more involved with someone who didn't deserve your love. He seemed to have so much influence on you. Suddenly nothing I said mattered and I'm afraid I overreacted."

She raised up to kiss him on the cheek. "It wasn't all your fault. I should have tried harder to explain. I can see now that if I had told you who Stephan was in the beginning, I could have avoided a lot of problems, but you always reacted so angrily when I mentioned him, I finally stopped talking about him altogether. Then when I decided Stephan and I would have to get married, there was a gap between us that I couldn't bridge. I think I was a little relieved when you wouldn't listen to me because I knew you would have tried to talk me out of it."

"You're damn right I would have," he said gruffly. "And I can't believe Stephan went along with your harebrained scheme."

"He reacted just about like you did at first," she laughed. "But eventually I convinced him that there was nothing legally or morally wrong with it. You have to remember he thought I was his real sister, but his birth certificate didn't name Daddy as his father and since we would be living as brother and sister, there would be nothing sinful about our relationship. And, of course, back in those days he was still resentful enough to feel that Daddy owed him something. So in the end, it wasn't all that difficult to convince him."

"Why didn't you just marry, then give him the money and get a divorce? Why did you drag it out for three years?"

"Because money wasn't the only thing he needed," she explained reflectively. "He wanted to be a part of the golden circle. I not only had the money, I had the right connections as well. All those girls I went to Hockaday with and Daddy's business associates. I was Stephan's ticket into the kind of life he thought he wanted."

"But you always hated that kind of life!"

"I know. Even so, it didn't seem too much of a sacrifice if it was what he wanted. You don't real-ize what his childhood was like. The bitch that raised him began filling him with spite from the minute he could understand what she was saying. He knew she only kept him around because she could use him to get more money out of Daddy." Arlie's eyes flamed, the muscles in her face tight-ening in anger. "And she didn't use a penny of it on Stephan. Daddy gave her the money to pay

Stephan's college tuition, but he had to get a scholarship in order to go."

"Arlie," Dan said quietly. "You had a deprived childhood, too. But you didn't turn into a thief and a vandal like Stephan. And you would never have let anyone make the sacrifices for you that you made for him."

"But Dan," she said in surprise, "I had you. Stephan had no one."

"Okay." He sighed. "You don't have to defend him. I suppose what you did was worth it. He's turned into quite a guy. A little zealous perhaps," he added with a grin, "but his head seems to be screwed on straight now."

"I can't take any credit for that," she objected. "I had hoped that he would get tired of playing games with those useless, frivolous people, but he didn't seem to see them in that light. Not until he met Connie. That was what turned him around. It was as though he suddenly saw the life he was leading through her eyes. And he definitely didn't like what he saw." She smiled in reminiscence. "He almost blew it with her though. She was too honorable to have an affair with a married man and he was too stubborn to tell her the truth about our marriage. So I told her myself. At least, I told her the truth as Stephan knew it. At first he was so smug, thinking he had charmed her into an affair, then he began to realize an affair wasn't enough. He wanted to marry her." She looked up at Dan and smiled. "So, we got an annulment and that's just exactly what he did."

"Didn't Connie think the whole thing was just a little bit strange?"

Arlie gazed at him pityingly. "You don't understand about women. Connie accepted it because she loved Stephan, too. If she had been in my position, she would have done the same thing."

He stood and walked across the room, his forehead creased in thought. "You're right about one thing. I don't understand women. The whole thing seems preposterous." He shoved his hands in the pockets of his jeans, turning to look out the window. "At least this explains your legion of lovers. Since Stephan thought you were his sister you couldn't have a normal marriage, so it was inevitable that you had affairs."

Oh, Dan, she thought, watching his stiff back, if you only knew. "Dan," she began hesitantly. "About that . . . I wanted to explain how—"

"You don't have to explain," he interrupted, his voice soft and sad. "You're a sensuous woman with strong needs." He turned to look at her over his shoulder, his mouth twisting with grim humor. "Your first lover must have gotten quite a surprise."

Arlie squirmed in embarrassment as he continued to watch her closely, waiting for her reply. How could she tell him? And how on earth could she expect him to believe her when she did? She glanced up and found his narrowed, probing eyes still trained on her face, a spark of comprehension forming as faint, warm color tinted her cheeks.

"Arlie," he said, a hint of a smile in his voice as he walked toward her. "You were a virgin when you married, weren't you?" Without waiting for her confirmation, he continued. "You had to be. I guarded you carefully enough. I thought I had slipped up with Stephan, but he wasn't interested in you in that way. And there was no one else, was there, Arlie?"

Hearing the amusement in his deep voice, Arlie eyed him malevolently, shaking her head to give the confirmation he no longer needed. He had it all figured out, but was enjoying himself enormously and was determined to drag it out for as long as possible.

He stood looking down at her, his arms folded casually, a wicked smile spreading his strong lips. "There's a lot of gossip in the crowd you ran with, isn't there? The men as well as the women. In fact," he leaned down to flick her nose with one teasing finger, chuckling as her lips tightened and her eyes flared, "some of them are even on the payroll of various scandal sheets. Right?" He lowered his voice to a conspiratorial whisper. "And you never know which one is a spy. You never know which one you can trust with . . . delicate information." He tipped her chin with one crooked finger. "Right, Arlie?"

Slapping viciously at his hand, she fumed, "You . . . you bastard."

"Tsk, tsk. Such language." He grinned widely. "One wouldn't expect that kind of language from a virg—"

"Don't say it!" she shrieked, jumping to her feet. "Don't you dare, Daniel Webster." At his shout of laughter, she doubled her fist and swung wildly at his chin.

Dodging the punch, he grabbed her fist as he stepped back. "What's the matter, darling?" He chuckled. "Surely you're not ashamed of being—"

"Dan," she warned tightly, her eyes blazing.

". . . a virgin," he finished cheerfully laughing again as she swung with her free hand.

"Oooh," she seethed through clenched teeth. "That word! It's a technicality, nothing more. A dark, insidious technicality, hanging over my head like an evil cloud. The *bête noire* that creeps around behind me, trailing me wherever I go."

"Poor Arlie," he said, pulling her unwilling body down with him to sit on the couch. "Trapped in your own lie. You couldn't have a lover without taking a chance on exposing your lie to a public who would have had a field day with the information."

"I suppose you think you're clever?" she muttered.

"No," he said, smiling at her disgruntled face. "But I know you. And I know you would do anything for Stephan. Including living like a nun to save him from malicious gossip." He pulled her head down to his shoulder, his voice softening. "Has it been bad for you, pest?"

Arlie sighed, curling her body into his comforting strength. "It's been hell," she said simply. "The sly remarks, the outright insults. Everybody thought I was Miss Hot Pants who would try anything once." She groaned. "Lord, Dan, if you only knew some of the propositions I've had in the last couple of years. Half the time I didn't even know what they were talking about. I mean," she raised her head, her tone injured, "I don't even know what a G-zone is and I haven't so much as seen a vibrating bed!"

"You poor, underprivileged thing." He laughed.

"I'm serious, Dan. But it was even worse when I *did* know what they were talking about." Her eyes widened as she looked at him in amazement. "Dan, you wouldn't believe what some of those people consider normal sexual practices."

"Yes, I would," he said, his face showing his distaste. "I just wish you hadn't had to deal with that sort of thing. Especially not alone."

"After a while it didn't bother me so much," she said, shrugging. "I would simply pretend that their most outrageous suggestions were boring. Which, naturally, added to my X-rated image."

"How in hell did you get that reputation in the first place?"

"It started out gradually. Just hints and insinuations," she explained. "About a month after we settled in Paris, Stephan fell head over heels for a sultry little French heiress. He didn't realize that people would start gossiping about his supposed infidelity. When they saw that his affair didn't leave me heartbroken, they assumed we had some kind of open marriage and that I was fooling around, too. It became a very popular game—trying to guess who Arlie was sleeping with."

"Stephan should be whipped for putting you in that position," Dan muttered tersely.

"He didn't know, Dan," Arlie defended. "He was dazzled by the glamour of a world he had always dreamed of. He just didn't see the decay and malice beneath the glitter. If he had known his actions would affect me, he would have gotten out immediately."

"So why didn't you tell him?"

"Because I didn't think it was necessary. I'm tough. And I had promised myself that I would do everything in my power to give Stephan the things he had missed out on as a child. Which includes caring enough about his happiness to take a few insults. It wasn't really that bad. At least it wasn't until the weekend I spent with Oscar Braun," she added ruefully. "Until then the rumors hadn't been public knowledge. They were confined to our immediate circle of friends."

"Braun? Isn't he . . ."

"The Swiss industrialist," she confirmed.

"My God, Arlie! He's got to be ninety years old. Why would you want to spend the weekend with him?"

"He's sixty-three," Arlie corrected. "And it wasn't my idea to spend the weekend with him . . . at least, not alone. I was invited to a skiing party along with twenty other people. Stephan was in Rome and you know how much I like to ski. I had heard from several people how beautiful and pic-

turesque Oscar's chalet was and I was excited
about going. Little did I know," she murmured.

"What happened?"

"Well," she said, leaning back against the couch
to draw her feet up beside her. "The first shock I
got was the ancient train that took me to a tiny
Swiss village. I was picked up at the station by a
very dignified German man driving a sleigh. It
was all very picturesque, just as promised, but
the chalet was actually a huge stone castle—a
little like Count Dracula's—and to make it even
more eerie, I found when I arrived that it was
completely empty. Except for the charming Herr
Braun."

Feeling Dan's muscles tighten, she patted his
arm in a consoling gesture. "I wasn't afraid," she
assured him. "He was a gentleman of the old
school and would never have forced himself on an
unwilling female, but I have to admit when I found
out he had cancelled all the other invitations, it
made me a little nervous. I knew I was in for a
weekend of hide and seek."

"Why in hell didn't you leave?" Dan asked angrily.

"How? We were miles from the village and there
was several feet of snow on the ground. On top of
that, it was dark and he had dismissed all the
servants, none of whom spoke a word of English."
She shook her head. "No, I was well and truly
stuck and I knew it. It wasn't as though I could
walk out and take a cab to the nearest motel. As I
said, I wasn't frightened, but Lord, that man was
tenacious. And surprisingly strong for his age."

"So what happened?" Now that he knew she
had not been harmed, Dan's voice began to lose
some of its stiffness.

"After dinner, he began to drink heavily. At first
I tried to slow him down. Then I decided that
letting him get drunk was probably the best way

out. I could have persuaded him very easily to leave me alone by insulting him, but I didn't see any need to injure the ego of an old man when he would probably pass out any minute. Which he eventually did."

She chuckled suddenly. "I thought I had it made then. I went on to bed, confident that I would be able to leave the next day with no more trouble from Herr Braun. I was just about to get into bed when he walked into my room, wearing the most ridiculous satin pajamas you've ever seen." She glanced at Dan as he drew in a sharp breath. "Don't worry. He just chased me around the room a couple of times and then passed out—on my bed. I found another bed, then the next morning, tiptoed back into my room, intending to pack and leave immediately. But unfortunately Sleeping Beauty woke up before I could even get out my suitcase." She hesitated, knowing the next part of her story would bring Dan's wrath down upon her head.

"And?" he prompted impatiently.

"Dan, you have to understand how he looked," she began earnestly. "He woke up and looked at me. At first there was a question in his eyes, then, slowly, a terrible look of defeat came over his face. Dan, I've never seen such emptiness in a man's eyes. It was as though he had shriveled up inside. I didn't understand why he felt such a sense of failure, but I certainly recognized it for what it was. How could I . . . how could anyone look at such suffering and not do something about it? It was such a little thing to me, but it meant so much to him." She raised her chin defiantly. "Even if I had known what the consequences would be to my reputation, I still would have done the same thing."

"What did you do, Arlie?" His voice was resigned,

his expression showing that he knew he was not going to like her answer.

"I lied," she said simply. "I made up a fantastic tale about how exciting he was in bed. I said he was the most wonderful, virile lover I had ever had."

"Arlene Frances Hunicutt," Dan whispered tightly, his fury building slowly to the final explosion. "You imbecile!" he roared, jumping to his feet to pace in front of her as Arlie flinched and covered her ears with her hands. "How could you pull such a stupid stunt? You're not fit to be allowed out without a leash. You've got no more sense than a . . ." He leaned over, shouting in her face. ". . . a cucumber!"

"How was I supposed to know the man hadn't made love in over a year," she muttered defensively. "Was it my fault he decided his renewed powers were due to my expertise? How did I know he would tell anyone who would listen that I was practically a pro?"

"Yes!" he boomed. "Yes, it was your fault. And you should have known his ego would demand that he spread it around. You were damned lucky he didn't keep you there for a replay."

"Well, he didn't," she shouted in return. "And I wasn't smart enough to know what he would do. And I told you, even if I had known, I would have done the same thing."

"Yes," he said, drawing back in amazement. "You would have. You would willingly subject yourself to the filthy innuendos of those vultures just to convince an old lecher that he could still get it up," he finished in disgust.

"Dan!" she protested. "Remember my innocence."

"Innocence, my foot," he snorted. "When I met you you were the only thirty-year-old first grader in history!"

"Come on." She laughed, pulling him down to sit beside her. "I made my bed of thorns and I didn't crab about lying in it. It got a little tiring after a while, I'll admit. After that weekend, I couldn't dance with a man without reading about our affair in the next morning's paper. No matter where I went, I was linked with whatever Don Juan happened to be in the area." She sighed in regret. "I had hoped that when I came home I could put all that behind me and start fresh, but it didn't happen that way. The legend of Arlie Fleming was already here, waiting for me to catch up with it."

"It's causing you problems here?" he asked, his eyes suddenly piercing. "Who's giving you trouble? Eric?"

"Not in the way you mean. It's just . . ." Now it was her turn to rise and pace. ". . . well, it's this virginity thing. You can't imagine what a handicap it is." She watched as his anger receded and unwilling amusement began to show in his eyes, his lip twitching slightly. "Well, it is. Every time I meet a man I like, I have to pretend he leaves me cold. I thought when I got back here, I could take care of it quietly, without anyone knowing about my marriage to Stephan. But everyone knows! And now, with Stephan and Connie living right here in the area, I'm caught in the same trap." She stopped the urgent flow of words to turn and look at Dan. "Stephan said the clinic was going to be written up in a major magazine and that he would have to represent the clinic when it came time to solicit new funds. He's going to be a public figure!" she said, her voice rising slightly. "I still can't take a chance on starting malicious gossip."

"You poor thing," Dan said, chuckling. "Doomed to a life of celibacy."

"It's not funny," she grumbled. "I'm beginning to get paranoid about the whole thing. I will never feel easy in my mind until I do away with this stupid virginity."

"And just how do you plan on doing that? Are you going to put on dark glasses and a wig and pick up a stranger off the street?"

"Believe me, I've considered it," she muttered. "But the idea just didn't appeal to me."

"By God, I should hope not."

"No, that wouldn't work at all," she said, ignoring the threat in his muttered words. "But, actually, I did have an alternate plan." She sat down on the couch and smiled up at him sweetly.

"Arlie," he said warily. "I don't like the look in your eyes. What are you planning now?"

"Dan, whenever I've had a problem, who always solves it for me?" she asked, gazing cheerfully into his suspicious brown eyes. "Do you remember when I cut my foot playing in the quarry? You cleaned it up and bandaged it for me because I would have gotten in trouble if anyone had found out. You've always taken care of me. And you've led me to believe I could always depend on you. In fact, one might say you encouraged my dependency," she accused slyly. "So it's actually your own fault that I'm having to rely on you . . ." she paused as the gist of her words began to sink in, ". . . to solve this one small problem for me."

Six

Arlie stared in fascination as Dan's face went through a series of comical expressions. First came bewilderment, his heavy eyebrows dipping low in a frown as his lips tightened. Then comprehension began to creep through, narrowing his eyes to piercing slits of suspicion before blank astonishment gave his lax features a stunned look. He stared into space, occasionally darting a look at her that seemed to search for other signs of insanity.

When his breathing became audible, his chest expanding and contracting as the fury built in visible stages, Arlie shrank back into the corner of the couch, tautening her muscles in anticipation of the inevitable blast. But, incredibly, his lips began to move silently and his breathing and color slowly began to return to normal. She relaxed with a relieved sigh as she realized he was counting.

Minutes later he turned to look at her, his face calm. "You want me to take care of this . . . uh . . . little problem for you," he said conversationally. "Is that right?"

She nodded silently, watching his unnatural calm warily. Dan had a very short fuse and she didn't relish the thought of another explosion. But apparently he had his anger well under control for he stood and casually walked to the fireplace, leisurely lighting his pipe before he turned back to her to continue their discussion.

"In other words, I'm supposed to break you in . . . like a new pair of shoes."

His voice was far too controlled and Arlie was almost relieved to see the flare of anger in his brown eyes as she laughed at his analogy. "No . . ." she began, then paused thoughtfully. "Actually, I guess that is what I mean, but you needn't sound like I just asked you to steal money from widows and orphans. After all, I could have taken care of the problem last night when you were in a drunken stupor and determined to get me in bed with you." She shook her head sorrowfully. "And a very disgusting display it was, too."

He ignored her teasing remark. "Why didn't you? Considering my condition, I probably wouldn't have known whether or not you were a virgin."

She smiled at his disgruntled expression. "I was tempted, believe me. But it wouldn't have been fair to you. You have the right to make a sane decision."

"Sane!" he shouted in disbelief. "You must be kidding. Sanity walked out the back door the minute you walked in the front." He ran his fingers through his unruly red hair and began to pace back and forth in front of the couch. "I had forgotten what it was like being around you. You're a jinx and trouble follows you like a shadow. Maybe I'm getting old, but I was enjoying my calm, orderly . . . *dull* existence. I had three years of relative peace, then you walk in and suddenly the very air is hyperkinetic. You sit there and smilingly ask me to deflower you like you were a six year old asking·to have her shoelaces tied. Just as though your lunacy were perfectly reasonable."

"Dan, Dan!" She sighed, shaking her head regretfully. "You're all hung up on the *idea*. Is it really so insane? I could have seduced you—don't deny it," she added as he gave her a sharp look. "You know I could have. And I could have thrown the anatomical facts at you at the last minute when it was too late to back out. Or I could·have let you discover it for yourself. But I didn't do that because we've always been open and honest with each other. You're simply upset because I said it out loud. Think about it for a minute. If some cute little thing started cuddling up to you, you would know immediately what she had in mind. You would consider it, then reject or accept her implied proposition. It would be the same thing. Except my way is more straightforward. Is an outright statement really more shocking than someone blowing in your ear and admiring your biceps? You still have the same options —to accept or reject as you wish."

He stopped pacing suddenly, standing before her, looking down at her in awe. "You're incredible," he murmured in amazement. "You could compare a Roman orgy to an afternoon tea party . . . and make the comparison sound logical!"

Throwing back her head, Arlie laughed at the distrust in his voice. "Poor old Dan." She chuckled. "I really didn't mean to throw you for such a loop. I should have let you get used to me gradually."

She stood and patted his arm sympathetically. "Why don't we shelve it for right now? You take your time and think about it. If the idea is still repugnant to you, then I'll simply have to formulate a new plan." She turned to leave, but found her arm locked in a rough grasp that halted her progress.

"Such as?" he demanded.

"Oh, I don't know," she replied airily. "But I'll come up with something." She smiled at him over her shoulder. "I always do."

As she left the room, she could almost hear the wheels whirring frantically in Dan's brain and she suppressed a pleased chuckle. That should keep him busy, she thought in satisfaction. He would drive himself crazy wondering what wild scheme she would concoct as an alternative. In the end he would give in and then Arlie would be ready to begin her new life, free at last from her inhibiting physical state.

For the rest of that day and the next, as Arlie threw herself into the search for employment, Dan kept a cautious distance between them. He worked in his studio during the day, frowning ferociously if she dared to interrupt him, and that night he kept her entertained with polite, impersonal conversation. But all the time he watched her as though he expected her to start frothing at the mouth at any moment. At times his attitude was so obvious she had difficulty keeping a straight face. She was almost tempted to jump out at him from behind a door, but somehow she felt he would welcome the excuse to blow up at her, so she squelched the impulse and pretended to be oblivious to the tension that grew steadily between them.

As Arlie gave her hair a final pat, checking her appearance in the full-length bathroom mirror, she decided that tonight, one way or another, she would have her answer. He had had plenty of time to come to a decision.

She turned to leave the bathroom, then stopped, frowning at her too-bright lipstick. Tonight she and Dan were attending a party given by the Prescotts and, remembering Dan's admonitions, she decided to change it for a more discreet hue. Picking up a muted beige shade, she began to apply a light coat.

"Arlie!"

"Damn," she swore, startled by the sound, then wiped a smear of lipstick from the corner of her mouth. As she walked out of her bedroom she muttered, "Sounds like a wounded water buffalo," then stopped just inside Dan's bedroom door and asked sweetly, "You bellowed?"

"Here. Do this," he said irritably, thrusting his right arm and a gold cufflink at her. He looked down at her as she deftly fastened his sleeve. "I just wanted to make sure you remembered what I told you about the Prescotts. No tricks tonight, please."

"Of course I remember," she said, stepping back to pick up his tie and hand it to him. "Look at me. Am I or am I not the picture of dignity?"

His eyes wandered down her body as he knotted his tie, taking in the sober string of pearls and the demure midnight blue taffeta dress. Her subdued makeup and sleek black hair, pulled back into a chignon from a center part, gave her the look of a modern madonna.

"Very nice," he said, his voice holding a touch of surprise. "I have to admit I'm impressed."

She cast her eyes demurely toward the floor, then looked up again, a sparkle appearing suddenly to lighten the blue eyes that had stolen the coloring of her dress. "Don't be too impressed," she whispered confidingly. "I'm wearing flesh-colored French underwear."

Drawing in a sharp breath, he closed his eyes and muttered, "I should have known." When he opened his eyes, the curiously aware look that had been present for the last two days was there again, but he simply turned away to pick up his jacket. "Let's keep that our little secret, okay?"

"I hadn't planned on announcing it to the general public." She laughed. "I just wanted you to know that I wasn't completely reformed."

"When pigs fly," he said, smiling against his will, "that's when you'll be reformed." He threw a friendly arm around her shoulders, more at ease with her than he had been since she had put her proposition to him the day before. "Come on, pest. It's time to go."

The party was in full swing when they arrived minutes later at the Prescotts' elegant suburban house. Arlie was captured as they walked in the door by an obviously admiring Eric and, while Diane took Dan to speak to her father, Eric began introducing Arlie to the friends and business associates who filled the large room to overflowing. Everyone she met, whether they greeted her with raised eyebrows or a knowing smile, made one thing painfully obvious—Arlie was known. Her reputation had preceded her once again, forcing her to resume the act she had grown weary of in the last three years.

Her discreet costume made no impression and was overlooked completely in favor of the more interesting rumors of her past. Very much in demand for gossipy conversation and not-so-subtle flirtations on the dance floor, she felt helpless against her reputation and was about to signal a watchful Dan for help when Eric maneuvered her away from her unwanted fan club.

As they joined the other couples dancing on the patio, Arlie breathed a sigh of relief. "Thanks, pal," she said gratefully.

"I couldn't let the unruly mob trample my prize, could I?" he asked, grinning impudently. "I'm saving you for myself, remember?"

"Whatever your reason, I'm eternally grateful."

"Oh?" he said, his eyes narrowing as they wandered suggestively down her body.

But Arlie missed the look in his eyes as she caught sight of Dan and Diane dancing companionably just inside the patio door. "They look nice together, don't they?" she murmured. "You'd think someone as large as Dan would look ridiculous beside a woman as small as Diane, but he doesn't. They look right."

Eric twisted to look over his shoulder and said, "You think so? Diane would be pleased to hear that."

Arlie glanced up, her eyes instantly alert. "Would she?"

"Yes, she would," he said, still looking at the couple in question. "She's always been fond of Dan."

"Everyone's fond of Dan," Arlie replied. "How fond is she?"

"I've wondered about that myself. Diane sees other men, but somehow I've always felt that Dan was special to her." He looked down at Arlie and smiled, his eyes filled with curiosity. "Diane tells me that Dan has always been a big brother to you. Is that all? He seemed awfully protective the other night. I was looking forward to our sail, but he seemed to think it would be a bad move."

"Dan has always thought he would do a better job of running my life than I would." She grinned. "And to tell you the truth, he probably would."

"But there's nothing between you?"

"We've got a lot of years and a lot of caring between us," she said softly, then looked up and smiled. "But if you're asking if we're in love . . . no, we're not. Dan sees me as a disruptive influence in his life. An albatross. He would probably murder me within a week if we were involved in that way."

"I have to admit, I can't imagine old sobersides being emotionally involved with someone like you," Eric said. "He's so . . . conventional. And even though some of his cartoons are pretty radical, the people he deals with—people like my father— are all conservative, too."

Arlie looked at Eric curiously. "Does your father think it's strange that I'm living with Dan?"

He glanced away uncomfortably. "He went a little stiff at first," he admitted, then smiled down at her. "But after Diane explained your relationship with Dan, he loosened up a bit." He pulled her closer, sliding his hands down to rest on her hips. "Now that we've disposed of Dan," he murmured, his eyes twinkling, "we can go on to more important things." He lowered his voice to a devilish whisper as he maneuvered her close to a row of potted plants. "You wanna fool around?"

Her eyes sparkled with laughter as she looked up at him. "You're salivating again." She reached down to pull his hands back to her waist. "Behave," she admonished.

He pulled her abruptly behind the row of greenery and Arlie prayed fervently that they were not visible to the people on the patio because Eric's hands slipped down again, this time to cup her rounded buttocks.

"You don't really mean that," he murmured, his fingers beginning a gentle massage of the firm flesh.

"Oh, no?" she asked, trying unsuccessfully to

remove his hands. "Eric," she said pleasantly, "this is your home. Your parents are standing less than fifteen feet away. How would you like for me to make a scene?"

"Ah, but you wouldn't," he said confidently, nibbling on her ear as he pulled her closer, molding her body to his. "You wouldn't take a chance on embarrassing old Dan."

She smiled. "If I slapped you and started screaming bloody murder, that might embarrass Dan," she admitted calmly. "And I might even come out of it looking like a shrew. In which case you would have the sympathy of everyone in the room and Dan's reputation could possibly suffer. But . . ." she drew back as far as his hands would allow and looked up at him with wide innocent eyes as she reached out to straighten his tie, ". . . that's not my style. When I get through with you, every person at this party will be looking at you as though you were Attila the Hun reincarnated."

Swallowing nervously, he said, "I don't believe you."

"Oh, no?" She looked over his shoulder at a couple who were passing on their way to the lighted pool area. Suddenly an agonized expression passed over her face and moisture welled up in her huge blue eyes. As Eric took a stunned step backward, tears began to trickle pitifully down each pale cheek.

"God!" he gasped. "That's enough. I believe you."

"Are you sure?" she asked, sniffing delicately. "If you need further proof, I've got a sob that would break your heart and it would be no trouble . . ." She let her voice trail off as she looked at him in inquiry.

"No!" he said, then added more calmly, "No, thank you. You've made your point."

Before she could decide whether or not to make him squirm, Dan appeared suddenly to stand beside her. He glanced sharply at Eric, then at Arlie, pulling a handkerchief from his breast pocket to casually wipe away her tears as he said quietly, "It's time to go, Arlie."

"But you just got here," Eric objected.

"I know. And I'm sorry we have to rush away, but Arlie has a splitting headache." Dan looked down at her. "Don't you?"

The look in Dan's eyes warned her not to contradict him. "Now that you mention it," she said, "I believe I do."

"I've already made our excuses to the Prescotts, so say goodnight to Eric," Dan said, taking her arm possessively, then barely gave her time to murmur a hurried good-bye before leading her across the room and out the door.

As they pulled out of the crowded, circular driveway, Arlie turned sideways in her seat to look at his strong face in the moonlight. "Why did I have a headache?" she asked with casual interest.

"Because I was sick of the place." He stared ahead silently for a few moments, then glanced over at her. "Whose idea was it to play slap-and-tickle behind the shrubbery?"

As she gazed curiously at the harsh, shadow-etched lines of his face, he reminded her suddenly of an old-fashioned fire-and-brimstone preacher. "Who do you think?" she asked quietly.

"You promised to behave," he murmured, almost to himself. "And you've never broken a promise to me before." Now his voice was stronger, containing a hint of laughter. "And judging by the look on Eric's face and the tears on yours, I'd say I interrupted one of your little . . . pranks." He glanced at her, a malicious grin spreading his firm lips. "What did the poor man do to deserve that kind of treatment?"

She gave him an indignant look. "The poor man

pulled me behind that overgrown artichoke and started to braille my derriere. How was I supposed to get out of there without drawing the attention of all your friends?"

"And I suppose you think no one saw you two hiding there?" he asked drily. "Every person in the place knew the exact minute you disappeared."

Drawing in a deep breath, she leaned back against the seat, feeling suddenly weary. "I'm sorry," she said slowly. "I didn't encourage him, Dan, but then it wasn't really his fault either. It's my blasted reputation. He knew I liked him and believed I would be . . . receptive." She threw him a startled look as a new thought struck her. "Is that why we left? Because I embarrassed you in front of your friends?"

He pulled the car into the driveway behind his house, killed the engine, then turned to look at her. "Don't be stupid," he said softly. "If any of my friends, business or personal, are offended because you want to snuggle behind the potted palms then that's their own business. It doesn't have anything to do with me."

She looked at him doubtfully. "Then why did we leave so suddenly? Honest, Dan, if my being here is going to cause problems for you, I'll leave. Connie and Stephan would let me stay with them. I don't want you to—"

"Shut up, Arlie," he said quietly. He opened the door and stepped out, stopping to add, "We left the party because I suddenly made up my mind to accept your proposition," then he shut the door in her stunned face.

"Oh," she murmured, her mouth hanging open vacantly, then scrambled from the car to follow him into the house. "Just like that?" she said to his broad back as he crossed the kitchen. "You've had two days to think it over and you wait until you're in the middle of a crowd to decide that you'll . . ." She hesitated.

He stopped in the hall and turned to look at her. "Deflower you," he finished for her.

"I wish you wouldn't use that word," she muttered irritably. "Deflower reminds me of defoliate which reminds me of Agent Orange which reminds me of insanity and so on and so on," she finished, waving her hand vaguely. "So don't deflower me. Lay me or screw me or . . ."

"Why don't we simply make love?" he asked, chuckling.

"Make love," she said, smiling slowly. "Isn't that a lovely phrase? 'Make' means bring into existence. Bringing love into existence must surely be one of the most worthwhile occupations in the world."

Dan leaned against the wall and looked down at her in inquiry. "If we're going to analyze it, I could get us a couple of chairs from the kitchen," he suggested.

"Oh. Sorry," she said, grinning. "Lead on, MacDuff."

Then as she followed Dan up the stairs, unreasonably her steps slowed and a strange knot of tension began to form in her stomach. What's wrong with me? she wondered in exasperation. This is what I wanted. I maneuvered and played my tricks and practically blackmailed him into this. And now I've won. I'll be free of my black cloud at last. She drew a breath into her painfully tight chest, coming to a halt to lean against the wall in confusion as Dan disappeared into his bedroom. So why am I hesitating now? she moaned silently.

"Arlie?"

She looked up to see Dan standing in the doorway, the soft light from the bedroom shining behind him. His face was obscured by darkness, but she didn't need to see him to recognize the amusement in his voice.

"If you're tired, I've got a chair and . . ." oh, yes, there was definitely a grin in his voice, ". . . a nice big bed for you to rest on. You don't have to stand out here."

She moved forward until she could see his face and began to examine it curiously. When did we switch roles? she wondered. When did I stop being the hunter and become the hunted instead? Am I like the dog who finally catches a cat and is suddenly faced with the problem of what to do with it?

Shrugging in resignation, she moved past him into the bedroom, knowing that she would not allow herself to back out now. She had never been a vacillator. Right or wrong she had planned her course and she would stick to it. When she stood in front of the bed, she turned, laughing nervously, ready to say something clever and breezy, then stopped as it suddenly hit her that this was Dan. Not a stranger to be impressed by her sophistication. This was the person who was closer to her than anyone else in the world.

She laughed in relief and sat abruptly on the bed. "Oh, Dan," she said wryly. "I feel like such a fool. I'm scared to death."

Chuckling softly, he joined her on the bed, pulling her close. "Fearless Arlie finally admitting to being afraid? I don't believe it." He leaned his chin against the top of her head. "Honesty like that deserves honesty in return. You're not the only one who is scared. I'm terrified."

She pulled back and looked at him in surprise. "You? Why, for heaven's sake? I've never done this before, but it's not exactly a new thing for you. You've done it plenty of times."

Drawing in a deep breath, he closed his eyes for

a minute. "But never with a virgin and never with you." He looked down at her, his face rueful. "You don't seem to realize what kind of burden you've put on me. This is not a surgical procedure we'll be performing here. The first time should be special. I don't want you to come away from this with bad feelings toward sex or . . ." he hesitated, sounding unsure of himself for the first time since she had known him, ". . . me. I don't want this to change our friendship."

"Dan!" she said, shocked. "Don't you know that nothing could do that?"

"No, I don't," he said. "And neither do you. Nothing is certain in this world. But I decided tonight that I can't let that hold me back. I've taught you all your life and this should be no exception." He grinned suddenly, his mood lightening. "At least I'll know you've been taught well."

"Conceited!" She laughed, then sobered to look up at him, her eyes clouding over. "Dan, if you're really worried about it, then, please, don't go through with this. I know it was my idea and I've treated it all like a game, but I can't help remembering the last time." She looked away uncomfortably. "That night in the gazebo," she said, then turned her head to look at him again. "You hesitated then, too. And afterward, you felt bad about what happened. You avoided me and felt uncomfortable around me when we did meet." She clasped his hand urgently. "Nothing can change the way I feel about you, but if our making love is going to make you . . . desert me again and feel disgusted with yourself, then let's call it off right now. Because I'd rather stay a virgin forever than lose your friendship."

"Forever?" he said doubtfully, his voice husky with some emotion other than amusement.

"Well, at least until I marry," she amended. "But you know what I mean."

"Yes, I know," he said softly. "Forget last time. It was a long time ago and I was a fool." His eyes grew dark and unfathomable as he added tightly, "I won't make the same mistake twice."

"You're sure?" she asked, her face filled with uncertainty.

"Positive," he said emphatically.

"So what do we do now?" she asked helplessly. "Should I change into something more comfortable or just strip down?"

"Whoa," he laughed. "Slow down. I suppose we should begin by getting used to touching each other."

"Okay, I'm game. What do you want to touch?"

"Come here, idiot," he said, drawing her back against him. Slowly he pulled the pins from her hair, letting it fall around her shoulders, and began to stroke the mass of ebony silk.

Arlie sighed and relaxed against him, waiting. But he simply continued to touch her hair softly and slowly. "This is very nice," she said drily. "But you've been patting me on the head since I was six years old—when do we get to the good stuff?"

"Arlie, you fiend," he said through clenched teeth, pushing her back on the bed and leaning over her to grasp her shoulders. "How am I supposed to seduce you if you're going to sit there critiquing my performance?" He smiled grimly. "There should be a law against making love to your best friend."

Was she his best friend? Somehow that sounded wrong. Dan had always been Arlie's best friend, but what had she ever given to him? She had never considered Dan's side of their relationship. She had always known Dan was her lifeline, her stability. But did he truly consider her his best friend? And if he did, why?

"Damn it, Arlie, where are you?"

His voice was rough with exasperation and Arlie blinked in confusion as she came out of her troubling reflections. "I'm sorry," she murmured contritely. "Where were we?"

He stared at her as she lay beneath him, her dark hair fanning out around her, and with a groan of frustration, he dipped his head to capture her lips.

Taken by surprise, it was a moment before Arlie felt any reaction at all. Then she was filled with a sweet, warm feeling of coming home and automatically parted her lips to deepen the sensation. His firm mouth moved slowly on hers, demanding nothing from her, but seemingly determined to ease her into pleasure. In a leisurely way his tongue explored the inner softness of her lips, then moved on to graze her teeth and tease the tip and sides of her tongue with his own.

Ending the exploration as slowly as he had begun it, he withdrew his tongue to outline her full lips, gently sucking her lower lip between his as he drew back until all that was left of the kiss was his warm breath on her tingling mouth and a delightfully boneless lethargy that drained her strength.

Lazily, she raised weighted eyelids to stare at him. His face was inches away and he seemed to be waiting for her reaction, his eyes filled with a peculiar wariness as though he were almost afraid of her response.

"That was . . ." She stopped to clear her throat. "That was fine," she whispered. Then as champagne bubbles began bursting in her veins, spreading an exhilaration throughout her body, she closed her eyes, moving her head sensuously against the silky spread and continued. "So fine," she murmured, a smile of satisfaction lifting her lips. She opened her eyes again and jerked her head sideways in a cocky beckoning motion. "More . . . more."

His laugh was short and relieved. "At least we know you're responsive. Not that I had any doubts," he added huskily. "You're a very physical woman, Arlie. You like touching and being touched." He raised his hand to smooth her long hair away from her neck. "And now it's time for the next step."

"Oh?" she whispered. He pulled her up and removed her string of pearls, then began to undo the buttons that ran down the front of her high-necked dress.

"Yes."

When he had loosened the belt at her waist and freed the last of the buttons below it, he paused, a fire beginning to burn deep in his eyes, then with hands that began to tremble slightly, he spread the dress wide, exposing her full breasts whose only covering was the sheer, almost invisible lace.

"God!" he breathed harshly. "When you told me what you were wearing underneath your proper little dress, the most vivid pictures formed in my mind, but nothing could compare with this."

Arlie felt her blood quicken as she heard his rasped words and she lifted her head to watch as he fumbled with the front of her bra, spreading it as he had her dress. Slowly, almost hesitantly, he touched the pebble-hard tip of one firm breast with a single extended finger, then moved to circle the tip of the other.

She gasped in pleasure as he took the weight of one smooth globe in his large hand, fascinated by the sight of his dark skin against the silken paleness of her own. Glancing up, she found he was watching her face with the same fascination.

"You're supposed to close your eyes and simply feel," he whispered, his voice deep and sensual.

"Oh?" she murmured, glancing back to the hand that smoothed and molded her breast. "I want to do it right, but . . ." she swallowed heavily, ". . . the sight of your hand on me is very . . . stimulating, isn't it?"

He laughed shakily, leaning his forehead against hers. "Stimulating is putting it mildly and I think it's time we moved on before I go completely crazy and scare the hell out of you."

He stood up, pulling her to her feet, and smoothed the dress down her arms, holding her as she stepped out of it. Her crisp half slip was discarded as quickly, leaving her standing before him wearing only the sheer French-cut panties and panty hose.

For a moment Dan seemed to have trouble controlling his breathing, his hand lifting toward her in a jerky motion, then his chest expanded as he inhaled deeply and he closed his eyes. When he opened them again, his breathing was steady and he moved her back toward the bed with an almost impersonal hand at her waist.

"Dan," she began hesitantly. "I know I'm new at this, but shouldn't you be undressed, too?"

"We'll get to it, sweet." He chuckled. "Do you have some dark, ulterior motive for wanting to undress me?"

"I don't think you could call it ulterior," she replied after considering the question, "but I've always wondered how you would look naked."

"Arlie!" He laughed, the disconcertion in his face showing that he hadn't expected her confession. "What a thing to say. Do you mean that all these years you've been mentally stripping me?"

"No," she said slowly. "At age sixteen I dreamed of you in armor." Her eyes began to twinkle as she sat down on the edge of the bed. "But by the time I was seventeen I was removing the armor."

"You're depraved," he said huskily, the wildfire kindling again in his eyes.

"I've always thought so," she said agreeably, then felt a tingling streak of electricity shoot through her veins as he began to unbutton his shirt and the teasing mood was lost in the sensual waves running between them.

He reached out to switch off the bedside lamp, then, as he saw the hunger growing in her eyes, changed his mind and pulled the shirt off, throwing it onto the chair that held her dress. By the time he had removed his clothes completely and came to her to gently remove the wispy panties and panty hose that were the only barriers left, the room seemed to resound with the sound of their labored breathing.

He turned away for a moment, then the room was filled with darkness and she felt the bed give under his weight. A delicious sense of anticipation filled her, concentrating in her heaving breasts and the lower part of her body as she waited to feel his warmth against her.

"We'll take it slow and easy," he whispered in her ear as he eased himself down beside her. "Are you nervous?"

"I don't think so," she murmured. "Am I supposed to be?"

"Not Fearless Arlie." He chuckled, then whispered huskily, his voice determined, "I'll make it beautiful for you, babe. I promise I will."

Then began a delicate seduction of the senses such as nothing Arlie had ever felt before. Dan set free emotions from within that she hadn't even known existed. In fact, she had spent most of her adult life repressing the feelings that he now drew so easily to the surface.

His hands, his lips, were everywhere, discovering every vulnerable spot on her body, making her tremble with pleasure, moan with delight. He slowly drove her wild with a tenderness that went beyond sensual hunger.

He seemed bent on tormenting her, giving her enough to make her head swim with pleasure, but not enough to satisfy the strange, new craving she felt. His hands never stayed long enough in one place for her to capture the incredible sensations. They brushed across her swollen breasts, the smooth, satiny skin of her stomach, then slipped lower, bringing a gasp, then a moan of desperation from her throat. His lips followed in the wake of his hands.

When he felt her fingernails digging frantically into his shoulders and her hips undulating beneath him in uncontrolled rhythm, he whispered, "Now you're ready, sweet. Hold on tight and I'll take you there."

She felt him pressing against her, felt his strength, his throbbing warmth between her thighs, then a sharp pain that momentarily took her breath away, but gave way to a wonderful sense of well-being and union.

Slowly he began to move—light, gentle strokes that allowed her passion to build again. But the languid pace couldn't satisfy Dan for long. She heard his labored breathing, felt the tenseness in his lean muscles, and each time she moved—to stroke his flesh, to brush against his body—a moan that sounded almost like pain was muffled against her neck, then just as she was beginning to feel a pressure, a driving ache in her loins, he attacked her body with a beautiful fury that left her panting. She held him close, afraid for a moment when the deep shudders shook his body. Then she saw his face and was filled with unbelievable pride and joy that she could have given him the fierce pleasure she saw there.

Rocking him in her arms she soothed him until his breathing returned to normal, then murmured, "Thank you, Dan."

He raised up on one elbow and ran his hand down her quivering body, sending a streak of fire through her veins. Leaning down to feather a kiss across her swollen lips, he grinned and murmured, "The opera's not over until the fat lady sings."

"I beg your pardon," she said, looking at him blankly.

"How do you feel, Arlie?"

"I feel fine. I'm not sore or anything if that's what you mean."

"No, that is not what I mean. How do you feel inside?"

"Oh, I don't know," she said irritably, unable to decipher his cryptic question. "I feel restless, kind of itchy. Is that how I'm supposed to feel?"

"At this point . . . yes. What you just experienced is the preliminary bout. Now we're ready for the main event." He rubbed his forehead against hers and said grimly, "If you still feel 'itchy' after that, I'll shoot myself."

Then with a stubborn look on his face he began his tormenting seduction again, teasing and taunting her body, sighing in satisfaction when he heard her responsive moans of pleasure. He tuned her body to the same feverish pitch, then entered her swiftly and surely, the feel of his warmth inside her pulling unimaginable emotions from deep within her. She shook with the power of the sensual explosions in her body. The sensations grew and grew until she felt she would burst with feeling.

Burying her perspiration soaked face in his neck, she begged him with unintelligible words to stop the torment, to release her from the perverse power that held her in its grip. When he moved a pillow beneath her hips, she wrapped her long legs around him instinctively, arching against him as his thrusts deepened and he moved his hand to place the heel in the curling triangle of hair that held the seat of her desperation.

He moved his hand gently against her and whispered hoarsely, "Let me have it all babe, your sweetness, your fire."

Then as though he had whispered a magic incantation, she felt the northern lights in her blood and she found her release in an incredible, shuddering explosion that rocked her very soul. She gave one gasping cry, then was lost to the world around her as she soared into a new and astonishing dimension of pure sensation, pure pleasure.

Seven

Minutes—or perhaps hours—later, Arlie surfaced from the sensual coma that held her in its grip and touched Dan's face where it lay against her breast. The touch was light and slow as though an abrupt movement might take away the miracle of what they had just shared.

She was hesitant to speak, but she had to tell him. She had to try to let him know what it had meant to her. Opening her mouth, she was non-plussed to find that no words came out. She cleared her throat to begin again, but when he raised his eyes at the sound, she knew that words weren't necessary. The same wonder, the same gratitude that she felt consuming her was contained in the warm brown eyes that looked up at her.

Closing her eyes, she pressed his face gently into her breast. "There are no words," she whispered, her voice barely audible, "but if it were physically possible for me to cry, I would be crying now."

A tremor ran through his body at her words and he turned to kiss the rounded flesh beneath him, then hauled himself up to lay beside her, pulling her into his arms. "I should have known," he whispered against her hair. "I should have known we would have something rare together . . . something to match our friendship."

"Yes, you should have," she accused softly. "I didn't know. Nothing I've ever read . . . nothing I've heard . . . *nothing* could have prepared me for that. But you knew. You've done it before so you knew what I've been missing all these years."

"No, Arlie," he said in a tone of hot denial. "You don't understand. I said something *rare* happened between us. If every time a man and woman slept together, something rare happened, it wouldn't be rare anymore. It would be ordinary. Men and women get together quite a lot you know," he added, his voice slightly amused.

"Yes, I know," she replied vaguely, her thoughts elsewhere. "Do you mean it won't ever be like this again?"

"Exactly like this . . . no. But between us," his voice emphasized the last word, "it will always be special. Things spark and catch fire when we come together."

"And that's what makes it special? Some kind of chemistry?" she asked, raising her head to rest it on her hand as she looked at him, curiosity filling her eyes.

He stared at her strangely. "Haven't you ever met anyone that you were drawn to physically? It's a kind of magnetism. You just know that things will click between you."

She considered the question for a moment. "You have to remember that I've spent the last three years avoiding anything physical. But even from before, I can't remember feeling like that." She frowned and sat up. "I've been mentally attracted. I mean, I've met men whose minds have fascinated me or who have been on the same wavelength . . . like Eric. And I've met men whose bodies I've admired—a well-developed thigh takes my breath away," she quipped, an impudent grin lifting the corners of her mouth. Then the grin faded and she looked at him with a worried frown. "Dan, do you suppose there's something wrong with me? I've never been physically attracted to anyone— except you, of course," she added, too distracted by her thoughts to notice his sharply indrawn breath. "In the last three years, whenever a man touched me, I was too busy wondering how I was going to stop it before things went too far to let myself feel anything. Maybe . . ." she looked at him with chagrin dimming her eyes, ". . . maybe I'm emotionally and physically stunted."

Dan began to laugh, the sound a mixture of delight and amusement, and pulled her down to rest on his chest again. "I can testify to the fact that you are definitely not stunted . . . emotionally *or* physically," he added, his hand cupping her full breast. "I won't swear to your mental capacity, but everything else works perfectly."

She grabbed a handful of curling chest hair, bent on punishing him for his disparaging remark, when her fingers encountered a golden bird. Lifting the sculptured figure, she looked up and said softly, "I'm glad you wear it."

He raised up to lean against the headboard, pulling her with him. "It's my good luck charm," he explained. "I've worn it since the night you gave it to me and it never fails me."

"Really?" she asked, her eyes crinkling with pleasure.

"Sure," he confirmed. "When bad luck comes along, it sees the gold chain and says, 'Poor man, he's got Arlie around his neck. He doesn't need any more trouble.' "

"Very funny," she said, disgruntled. "That was not exactly what I had in mind when I gave it to you."

For a few moments a heavy silence filled the room and she wondered what was going through his mind, then he turned her head toward him with a hand against her cheek and said slowly, "I think it's time we talked about that night, Arlie."

"Do we have to?" she sighed, unwilling to do anything that might lessen the closeness between them. "We came through it with our friendship intact, so I don't see any need to rehash it now." She paused. "It's strange, but all that seems so far away. Not the actual incident, but the maneuvering behind it. The same maneuvering I used this time. All those games and the way I looked at life. It all seems so . . . foreign now." She smiled at him. "I think I've grown up at last."

His hand tightened on her face. "Not too much. Don't grow up too much, Arlie." His voice held a peculiar intensity. "You have a capacity for joy—an openness to life—that most of us lose somewhere along the way. The truth is, I don't think I ever had it to lose, but somehow when I'm with you, a little of it rubs off on me."

The poignancy in his voice hurt her suddenly and she lifted her hand to smooth the lines from his forehead. Poor Daniel. He had been a grave, thoughtful adult at fourteen when she had first met him. He had gone to work to help support his family when he was twelve, then had been father to Arlie as well as to his own brother and sister. His mother had come to depend on him to keep the family together and Dan had never questioned the responsibility he had assumed on his father's death. He simply accepted it as a part of his life, readily taking Arlie into his care when she came his way by chance. He had been so busy with his responsibilities, he had never learned to enjoy himself. The thought of the boy he had been, the thin shoulders that had carried so much, made her chest tighten painfully.

"There was no time for you to be a little boy," she whispered. "If you'll teach me responsibility," she added harshly, "I'll teach you how to be a fool."

"No, not a fool," he objected softly. "Don't feel guilty for enjoying your life. It's what I wanted for you. And don't imagine that our friendship in some way added to my problems. I don't regret my life. Responsibility has its rewards, you know. I would have had a very dull life without you popping up to shake me. And I've had tonight," he whispered huskily. "Of course, there are also drawbacks. Which brings us back to that night in the gazebo." His eyes darkened and his expression became determined. "I want to explain about that night, Arlie. I know I hurt you and I want everything out in the open. I don't want that event between us in any way now. When you came to me that night, you were the loveliest thing I had ever seen. I wanted you, Arlie." His arms tightened around her when he heard her muffled gasp. "But you've got to understand my position. I knew you were trying out your wings. Testing your femininity. I couldn't use your vulnerability to get what I wanted. It wouldn't have been fair to you. You were so damn trusting. You had always followed wherever I led you. I simply couldn't lead you into something that might harm you. My responsibility to you wouldn't let me."

The depth of his caring touched her as deeply as his lovemaking had and she found she couldn't speak. What could she possibly say to him? She didn't deserve that kind of care. She had frivolously skipped through life while Dan had been living it. All the times she had done things to cause him worry came flooding back to depress her with the enormity of her thoughtlessness. She slid out of his arms and off the bed to stand in front of the window, pulling the curtain aside to stare with unseeing eyes into the moonless night.

"Arlie?" His voice was hesitant as he came to stand behind her. "You understand, don't you?"

"Yes, I understand," she said tightly. "I understand that I was a thoughtless little bitch back then." She turned to face him, her eyes shining with urgent purpose. "But never again, Dan. This won't ever be a one-sided friendship again." She clasped his hand tightly between both of hers, her words a vow. "I *will* be your best friend from now on, I promise."

"Arlie!" he grated out harshly, pulling her into his arms, surrounding her with his familiar warmth. "Don't think I blame you for what happened. It was a perfectly natural thing and I screwed it up royally. Your face—so pale and hurt—has haunted me for years. I knew how insecure you were underneath the brashness. And I'm afraid I added to that insecurity. I never want to see you look like that again."

She moved her face against the soft hair of his chest. "Yes, I hurt. I've never wanted to cry so badly. But not because of what you did. Because of what *I* did. I was afraid I had spoiled things between us."

"Then we're both idiots," he said. "Because you were right, nothing can spoil things between us." He moved his hand to her neck, his thumb lifting her chin so he could see her face. "Does it still bother you . . . not being able to cry?"

"Yes," she said, shrugging casually to hide just how much it bothered her. "But I don't spend a lot of time regretting it. It would be a waste of time." She drew in a deep breath, stepped back from him and smiled. "Not like our activities tonight. Now that is what I call time well spent." She started to continue on the same teasing note, but stopped as her pulse began to race at the sight of his naked body. "Nice thighs," she murmured, then shook her head and continued with her original thought. "You have equipped me with the ability to meet the world of male-female relationships with confidence. And a very enjoyable process it was, too."

He turned abruptly away from her, gazing out the window as she had moments before. "So you think you're ready now to tackle an affair with, say . . . Eric?" he asked, his voice low.

Eric? Why did that sound wrong . . . feel wrong? She twined her arms around her waist, unsure of herself suddenly. "Well . . . sure," she said hesitantly. "Sure, I am." She stepped closer in confusion. "Aren't I?"

"You know what they say." He looked at her over his shoulder, his eyes veiled. "It takes more than one swallow to make a summer. Think about it a minute. You're supposed to have slept with every able-bodied man in Europe. Unless you're very dense you would have to pick up a few tricks in the midst of all that debauchery." He turned around, shaking his head as though he regretted having to disillusion her. "You make up for a lot in enthusiasm, sweet, but experienced you're not. The first man you sleep with will recognize instantly that you're a novice at the sport of kings."

"He will?" she murmured, her eyes brightening unexplainably.

"Sure, he will," Dan said cheerfully, placing a consoling arm around her shoulder. "What you need is practice before you go out on your own."

"You really think so?" she asked, looking at him with suspicious eyes. "I have to admit it makes sense. What you're saying is I need to learn the . . . um . . . tricks of the trade, so to speak."

"Right," he confirmed, his voice serious, his eyes twinkling with amusement.

"And of course, you—being a man of the world and all that—will be able to teach me the things I need to know."

He placed a solemn hand over his heart. "I promise I'll give you the full benefit of my vast experience."

"I'll just bet you will," she muttered, laughter bubbling up inside her. She loved to see Dan teasing. Maybe she gave him something after all. "You're an unscrupulous scoundrel," she laughed. "You just want a nubile young body to warm your tired old bones."

He jerked her laughing form against his body, leaning down to nuzzle her neck. "My bones are not the only thing you warm. Now, I think it's time to continue your education."

"I'm ready, professor," she murmured, tilting her head to allow him better access to the sensitive skin of her neck. "Anything except position number thirty-eight," she whispered lazily. "Standing on my head makes me nauseous."

He chuckled, pulling her toward the bed. "You're not ready for the more exotic positions yet. You have a lot to learn about the basics first and I'd better warn you, your education is going to be slow and very thorough."

"Oh, well," she said, unconcerned. "I always say if you're going to do something, do it well."

"A wise philosophy," he murmured softly as they sank together onto the bed.

Arlie slowed her swinging stride to a crawl as she neared the house. The mid-afternoon sun beat heavily on the top of her head, but she had grown up in this sun and it wasn't for that reason her pace slowed. Procrastinator that she was, she was putting off the explanation she knew Dan would demand when she walked in the door.

Leaning against a brick planter which stood next to the sidewalk, she grimaced as she looked down at the smudge on the skirt of her green silk shirtwaister. The bus ride home had been an exercise in chaos. The bus's air conditioning system had been on the blink and as a result, the children of the midday shoppers had begun a mini-revolution. Since Arlie had fully expected them to hijack the bus for a side trip to Cuba, she felt lucky to have survived the experience with only an artistically placed chocolate handprint on her skirt.

Feeling the tickle of movement on her hand, she glanced down to find she had blocked the main thoroughfare of a colony of busy ants. She watched as three of the tiny titans struggled to carry a monumental bit of potato chip across her hand. Their strength and perseverance amazed her. The unwieldy bit of chip towered above the small black creatures, but they didn't give up. She could almost hear an invisible foreman shouting orders to the scurrying laborers as they pulled here, pushed there and investigated a snag in the rear. Not exactly a rubber tree plant, she thought, but an impressive feat nonetheless. She lifted her chin in determination, chuckling as she wondered how many people received silent pep talks from ants.

"Arlie?"

Even though she hadn't heard Dan's approach, she was not startled by the sudden sound of his voice next to her. She looked up at him and smiled. "Hi," she said softly, pleased by the sight of him.

He stared at her for a moment, a hint of laughter showing around his crinkling eyes. "Why are you standing out here in the heat?"

"I'm watching the ants." She glanced down at her hand to find that the three indomitable workers had conquered the summit of her hand and were moving on to blaze new trails. "They're fantastic," she murmured. "It makes you wonder what they eat for breakfast."

"I see," he said his eyes widening with enlightenment. "You left work early so you could come home and watch the ants."

Her lips twisted in a whimsical smile as she straightened, pulling away from her brick support. "Would you believe the president of the company decided they had made enough money today and let everyone go home?"

Placing an arm around her shoulders, he moved her steadily toward the house. "No, I don't think I would."

"I didn't think so," she sighed in resignation. "I was fired."

He chuckled softly. "I told you not to fib about your typing speed."

"Oh, it wasn't that. I haven't even seen a typewriter. I've been filing and xeroxing and running errands all week."

Opening the front door, he ushered her inside. "So what did you do to get yourself fired after only three days?"

She walked into the living room, stepping out

of her shoes on her way to the couch. "Remember that girl I told you about? The one with the new baby," she asked over her shoulder.

"What does she have to do with you losing your job?"

"It's a long story," she sighed. "You'd better sit down while I tell you."

When he had eased himself down beside her, muttering, "That bad, huh?" she took a deep breath and began. "Her name is Anna Martinez and she just hated leaving her baby all day with a sitter, Dan," Arlie explained fervently. "The company doesn't hire part-time employees, but I remembered reading about a job-share plan that has been tried successfully. That way she could keep her seniority. So . . ."

"So . . . ?" he prompted.

"So I went to the personnel manager to explain the plan to her, but she said she didn't make the company's policies, she only carried them out. So . . ."

"So?" he repeated impatiently.

"So I went to see the president—on my own time," she assured him. "I figured he would be able to get the policy changed." She frowned. "And he could, too. But he didn't want to." Looking up at Dan, she added, "Mr. Blair is not what you would call an altruistic man."

"He fired you for making a suggestion?"

"No—o—o," she said hesitantly, "not exactly. I think he fired me because I called him a stick-in-the-mud, obdurate, self-approbating old poot, but of course I could be wrong. It might have been something else entirely."

Dan choked suddenly as though the shout of laughter she saw in his eyes had become lodged in his throat. He swallowed an enormous gulp of air and said calmly, "You called him a stick-in-the-mud . . . etcetera, etcetera . . . because he wouldn't accept your suggestion?" She nodded. "And he took exception to that?" he asked incredulously. "The man is obviously too sensitive."

"I know what you're thinking," she said irritably. "You think it's all my fault because I couldn't hold my tongue, but you don't know what provocation I had. He wouldn't even consider the job-share plan. 'Ms. Fleming,' " she mimicked. " 'Our present policy has worked very well for years. We mustn't tamper with success.' "

She looked up at Dan, her eyes blazing. "And that's not all. When I tried to explain the benefits to the company, he called me a bossy little bitch," she fumed. "Now I'll concede that I'm often bossy and at times even a bitch, but, Dan, *little*? That was a deliberate chauvinistic slur."

He gathered her into his arms, a tremor of laughter vibrating through his body, and murmured, "My poor little—sorry—my poor *big* darling. You're simply not cut out to be a gofer. You're too accustomed to giving orders to take them without question."

"It's not that, Dan," she objected heatedly. "I can adapt to anything. They hired me to be a gofer and I was a damned good one, but how can you see that kind of stupidity and antediluvian attitude without trying to do something about it?"

"You keep your mouth closed and work within the system for changes," he said patiently. "Being a crusader is fine, Arlie, but being an effective crusader is even better. You'll have to learn to control these wild impulses." He dipped his head to gently nip her ear. "At least at work. Here at home you can be as wild and impulsive as you want." He tilted her chin, his lips twisting in a crooked smile. "Don't I get a hello kiss?"

"You're very distracting," she complained softly. "How can I formulate a plan to wipe out the world's injustices when my brain turns to silly putty every time you touch me? Is that what you want? A mindless slave to passion?"

"I just want you," he said gruffly, freeing the top button of her dress. "It's been too long since we made love, sweet. I'm hungry for you."

"We made love a few hours ago. Just before I went to work," she reminded him, her voice husky, her hand suddenly unsteady as it slipped inside his shirt.

"That's too long," he whispered seconds before his mouth fastened on hers with greedy impatience and suddenly the greatest injustice Arlie could imagine was the thought of having to leave his arms for a single moment . . . then there was no room for thought, only sensation after incredible sensation.

Later however, when she lay across the bed, filled with the glory and the peace that loving Dan always brought, the questions returned. Rolling lazily onto her stomach, she propped her chin in her hands as she watched him dress. "What am I going to do? About Anna and about a job?"

He glanced toward her, smiling as he studied the long line of her bare form. "About Anna— nothing. She's a grown woman and you can't live her life for her. She'll either find a job that suits her better or work to change the one she's got." Tucking in his shirt, he began fastening his belt as he moved closer to the bed. "As for a job . . . I have something in mind that we can talk about later." He sat on the bed, pulling her into his lap. "Has anyone ever told you that you've got a cute tush?"

"Cute?" she queried, raising her eyebrows regally.

"Is that supposed to be a compliment? You should say something about my classic lines or the elegance of my shape."

"Classic and elegant don't make me want to grab a handful. Cute does."

She grinned, twining her arms around his neck. "Then I guess I'll settle for cute." Suddenly she sighed and leaned her head against his shoulder. "Can't we talk about the job now? Jobs are hard to find, even for qualified people. I've got to find something and start supporting myself."

"Why?" he asked, gazing over the top of her head at a vision only he could see. "I know you want to do something with your life, but what's the rush? I'm not exactly poor, you know. I'm sure I could feed you until you get proper training."

Arlie raised her head and looked at his solemn face with curiosity shining in her purple velvet eyes. "Do you mean you want to support me while I go to school?" Her eyes sparkled suddenly as she became intrigued by the idea he had presented. "You want me to be your mistress?" A wicked smile curled her lips. "I would be a kept woman. That sounds so deliciously wicked," she chuckled, then sighed and shook her head. "No, I guess it wouldn't work. I'm determined to make my own way. I promised myself I wouldn't be a liability to you ever again."

She stood up and pulled on her robe. "But that's not the only reason. I need this for me. I have to *do* something. You've always had your work. You don't understand what it's like to be useless." Her chin lifted in determination. "I will not be a mistletoe."

"You idiot," he said in amused exasperation. "I wasn't suggesting that you become my mistress. I was, in my own fumbling way, offering you a loan. You could go to one of the community colleges without worrying about your work schedule, then in four or five months, when you're flush again, you can pay me back. I'll even charge interest if you like."

"A loan?" she murmured thoughtfully. "And I could pay you back in a few months?" Her expression lightened. "That would be perfect." She looked at him suddenly, her brow wrinkled in thought. "Does that mean you don't think I would make a good mistress?"

"You would make a delightful mistress," he assured her, chuckling. "But if you were around the house all day, I would never make the deadline on that damnable cartoon strip." He stood, pulling her into his arms, and kissed the tip of her nose. "Speaking of which, I'd better get back to what I was doing before you came in and dragged me—against my will—into the bedroom."

"I simply don't have your willpower," she laughed, then followed him slowly down the stairs, biting her lip as she turned over his proposal in her mind.

"Dan," she called as he walked toward his studio. "What courses could I take in college? Shouldn't I have a direction in mind before I start classes?"

He turned back and leaned against the bannister. "It's not absolutely necessary. You can always decide after you get started. Just see what hits you," he said. "But isn't there something that you really enjoy doing? Something you think you'll be good at?" When he saw the twinkle in her eyes, he laughed. "We've already ruled that out as a career possibility, remember? How about photography? Those snapshots you sent me while you were in Europe were remarkably good."

"Photography?" she mused, sitting on the bottom step as she considered it. "I love it, but there wasn't anything exceptional about those pictures. They were the same stuff every tourist brings back."

"No, you're wrong," he contradicted emphatically, joining her to sit on the stairs. "Whether you know it or not, you had some beautiful character studies in those snapshots. The one you did of that old Italian man looking out over his fields was one of the most moving things I've ever seen. It was as though he were awed and a little surprised by the beauty of it all. Beauty that only he could see."

"But the lighting was bad in that one," she objected, "and it came out a little fuzzy. I don't even know how to adjust a camera for those things."

"That's a technical detail, Arlie. It doesn't have anything to do with the sensitivity behind the composition of the picture. And your natural ability to recognize a good subject. Don't you know that most talented people fail to recognize their own talent? It's so natural to them, they assume it must be natural to everyone."

She looked at him thoughtfully, mulling over his words. "If you say so," she said, still a little skeptical of this talent he claimed she possessed. "Anyway, it will give me a place to start and it's definitely something I'll enjoy." She stood up, tightening the belt on her robe. "Now go back to work and stop sitting around on the stairs gossiping. Don't you know procrastinators never prosper?" she scolded.

"Yes, ma'am." He chuckled, disrespectfully patting her on the rear as she turned to leave him.

In the kitchen, as she began her preparations for dinner, she smiled ruefully when she realized that once again Dan had pointed her in the right direction.

"When am I going to stop depending on him?" she asked the frozen sirloin. But it seemed that the taciturn cut of beef found the question as difficult to answer as Arlie herself did.

Eight

Arlie never knew exactly when she first realized. It could have been in the back of her mind since the night they made love for the first time, surfacing gradually with each passing day. Or—being dense as Dan called her—perhaps realization had come all in a lump the day she watched him at his drawing board with the sun streaming through the window behind him, setting a torch to his auburn hair, highlighting the fine, red-gold hair on the back of his deceptively awkward looking hands as they maneuvered a pencil with swift dexterity across his sketch pad.

But whenever or however it came to her, Arlie knew now what she should have known years ago. She was in love with Dan. Not as a brother or a friend . . . as a man. It had always been Dan— from the first moment she met him. Perhaps that

was why her love had been so difficult to recognize—because it had always been with her.
There had been no startling revelation. No blinding flash of emotion. Loving Dan was as natural
to her as breathing. What had begun when she
was only a child had matured slowly through the
years, growing and swelling until, by the time
they met in fierce passion, it had filled every pore
and cell that made her Arlie.

When the truth finally caught up with her, she
wanted to shout it to the world. To stop strangers
on the street and share her discovery with them.
But most of all she wanted to tell Dan—the one
person she couldn't tell. Because, as unbelievable
as it seemed to Arlie, the same truth had not
caught up with him. He wanted her as his lover,
but not his love. To him she would always be an
albatross, his special burden. So she had kept her
love to herself, hugging it close when it threatened to spill over. Knowing Dan, he would have
believed it was in some way his fault. And conse-
quently the responsibility he felt toward her would
have grown.

Curiously, the fact that he didn't love her in the
same way she loved him didn't make Arlie unhappy. She knew he cared for her in his own way
and, for now, it was enough. Her love brought her
such intense joy, there was no room for sadness,
no time for wishing for the impossible.

Arlie smiled slowly, closing her eyes as she rested
her head against the end of the tub. Raising her
foot slightly, she felt the pink bubbles sliding on
and around her toes. She had always considered
herself a sensual person, enjoying the sights and
sounds and feel of the world. But now she knew
that she had been trapped in a shadow world
before Dan freed her senses. The world around
her had taken on a new and wonderful clarity.

She could feel the air sliding around her body as she moved. Taste the dawn minutes before it came. See the song of a bird as it fell on the ears of a child. She was alive, really alive.

"Arlie, have you seen my . . ."

When the rest of the question was not forth-coming, Arlie opened her eyes slowly. Dan stood in the open doorway of the bathroom taking in the lazy picture she made as she reclined in the tub. Moving forward, he reached down to scoop up several bubbles and dab them on her nose with one long finger. "Why are you sleeping in the tub when we're supposed to be at my mother's house in . . ." he glanced at his watch, ". . . less than an hour?"

"I'm dreaming dreams," she murmured, her eyes drooping lazily. "Weaving visions of incredible beauty . . ." She opened her eyes wide and raised one small foot. ". . . and soaking the calluses off my heels."

Chuckling, he turned to leave the room. "That's what you get for going barefoot all the time."

"Dan?" she said quietly, stopping him before he reached the door.

He paused, glancing back over his shoulder to give her a questioning look.

"Have I seen your . . . what?"

His forehead creased with thought for a moment, then he looked down at his feet, bare on the tiled floor, and said, "My socks. I can't seem to find my socks."

"I moved them," she said cheerfully, rising to wrap the fluffy pink bathsheet around her drip-ping body as she stepped from the tub. "I was making a statement."

"What kind of statement can you make with socks?"

"A very effective one apparently," she said, bending to rub her long legs dry. "This is the third time you've asked me where they are. Every time you need socks, you come to me," she said, her eyes crinkling with laughter that was hidden by her bent head. "Which means you think about me more often."

Straightening, she glanced at Dan to continue teasing him, but judging by the look on his face, she doubted he had heard a word of her ridiculous banter. His eyes were moving restlessly over her body, his face containing—not the amusement she had expected—but a confusing mixture of emotions. Desire was there certainly, flaming deep and bright in his eyes. But separate from the desire was a hunger that had nothing to do with sex. There was also frustration. Or perhaps it was impatience. Whatever it was, it was cutting into his peace, disrupting his thoughts.

"Dan?" she whispered, moving closer, concern showing in her furrowed brow and puzzled frown.

With a strange groan deep in his throat, he pulled her forward into his arms. He buried his face in her throat, muttering unintelligible words as he released her topknot with jerky movements.

"Dan?" She pushed at his shoulders, leaning back so she could see his face. "Dan, did you say 'aargh'?" she asked, her lips twitching with a combination of uncertainty and amusement.

"Yes," he replied heatedly, gripping her shoulders to give her a quick shake. "That's exactly what I said . . . aargh!" he repeated, releasing her to run his fingers through his hair as he stepped back into the bedroom and began to pace. "You're driving me crazy. I can't keep my mind on my work, I can't find my socks, and now I'm beginning to talk like one of my damned cartoon characters."

Sighing deeply, she leaned against the doorjamb,

all trace of amusement gone as she watched his exasperated strides. "There is a solution, you know," she offered quietly.

"No!" He stopped pacing to turn and glare at her. "We've discussed this before and we agreed you would stay here until you start receiving your allowance again. And that's more than three months away." He closed his eyes and repeated harshly, "Three months." Taking a deep, shuddering breath, he opened his eyes and continued, his voice calm. "Just forget what I said. I've got . . . things . . . on my mind."

Moving forward, he reached out to place his hands on her bare waist and pull her to him. "I'm sorry," he said contritely, giving her a coaxing smile as he kissed her briefly on the forehead. "I didn't mean to be such a bear. Forgive me?"

"Of course I do, you fool," she said, smiling to hide how deeply his mood disturbed her. And not for the first time. In the last few weeks, Dan's behavior had grown progressively more erratic, swinging from euphoric happiness to explosive exasperation without warning.

Giving him a quick squeeze, she pulled away to move toward the closet. "And now to track down the elusive socks." She switched on the light and pulled out one of the drawers that was built into the large closet. "Aha! The tricky little devils are here. Right where you told me to put them."

"I did, didn't I," he admitted sheepishly as he selected a pair. "So there would be room for your things in the bureau."

"Uh-huh," she confirmed smugly. "Would you like me to pin a note to your shirt so you'll remember next time?"

"Senility is not a laughing matter, Arlie," he chided cheerfully as he walked back into the bedroom, his mood swinging once again. "By the way . . ." he paused to give her an all encompassing look, ". . . when I said not to dress for dinner at Mom's, this was not exactly what I had in mind," he said, indicating her lightly tanned, nude body.

"I'm not through dressing," she said airily, pushing him out of the way to walk to the walnut bureau. "I have a pair of beaten gold earrings that I thought I would wear."

His laughter lingered long after he had left the room, staying with Arlie as she dressed carefully for her first encounter with Sarah Webster in many years. She admitted to herself that she was more than a little nervous about tonight's meeting, but overriding that nervousness was her concern for Dan. He had left her alone to dress for the first time since they had become lovers. Normally he sat watching her with a look of fascination on his face, seemingly intrigued by her every movement. He watched her intently while she performed the most trivial tasks, from painting her toenails to arranging her hair.

The first time Arlie had mentioned finding a place of her own, Dan had reacted wildly, throwing her to the bed with a violence that was just barely subdued. Although he hadn't harmed her in any way—it wasn't in Dan to do physical injury to someone weaker than himself—he had made love to her with a desperation that hadn't allowed for the removal of their clothes. Instantly consumed by the desperation in his urgent caresses, she had met each thrust with a driving hunger that brought them quickly to an explosive climax. And somewhere in the midst of the convulsive pleasure, she had heard him gasp harshly, "Don't you see, it *couldn't* be better than this."

Later she had gone over the barely audible words again and again, but could not discover the reason behind them. Was he trying to convince her . . . or was he trying to convince himself? What was behind his bewildering mood swings? If it had something to do with her presence in his house, why didn't he let her leave? And if it were something else, why, for heaven's sake, wouldn't he talk to her about it?

As she gazed in the mirror at the studied casualness of her long, sleek ponytail, her full-sleeved sapphire blouse and crisp white linen skirt, she knew the picture was marred by the look of worry on her face. Dan had always found it difficult to talk about his personal problems and now was certainly no exception. He helped all who came to him with their problems and, as a result, years of being the strong one, the one on whom everyone leaned, had made him automatically thrust his own problems out of sight.

Arlie had gone over endless possibilities for an explanation. She knew his cartoon strip had been accepted with gratifying enthusiasm, so his behavior couldn't be caused by artistic temperament or pressures of work. The possibility that had been the most acceptable was Diane. Acceptable as a viable explanation, not acceptable to Arlie's peace of mind. She fought the thought of his brooding over another woman, even one as nice as Diane, but she had promised herself she would be a true friend to Dan and do anything she could to make him happy. So if Diane was what it took to make him happy, then Arlie would do anything in her power to see that he got her.

But on the other hand, she thought, allowing her resolve to weaken, Diane couldn't possibly explain all of his behavior. On at least two occasions Dan had made flimsy excuses to keep Arlie at home instead of accompanying him to dinner parties. Diane had not attended either of the parties. She had called or stopped by on both occasions, so she couldn't have had anything to do with his strange behavior on those nights. Several times, friends of Dan's had called before dropping by and Dan had put them off with ridiculous excuses. He had explained his behavior to Arlie by a teasing reference to her continuing education and lectured her on the benefits of dedication. But beneath his teasing, Arlie could see that he was troubled and she was worried about him. Somehow she had to get at the truth.

His passion for her hadn't dimmed in the least, so it couldn't be that he was tired of her. He still reached for her eagerly each day when she returned from her classes at the community college. He was unceasingly thoughtful, incredibly caring . . . but something was wrong. And no matter how many times he denied that she was the cause, Arlie couldn't quite believe him.

Jerking up her purse in a swift, frustrated motion, Arlie left the bedroom, standing for a moment at the top of the stairs to allow the worried look to slide from her face, replacing it with a serene smile. Then she ran down the stairs to join Dan.

He looked at his watch as she entered the living room. "My, my," he said, his thick eyebrows raised in astonishment. "You've left us fifteen whole minutes for a thirty minute drive. This is the closest you've ever come to being on time."

"Let's not get tacky," she chided. "Just call your mother and explain that we'll be a little late."

"I did that when she invited us," he said smugly.

"You think you're so smart, don't you? One of these days when I'm a famous photographer, you'll come to me on your hands and knees to beg my forgiveness for all your insults." She gave him a haughty look. "And I'll say 'Daniel who?' "

Dan was still laughing as they climbed into his car and although Arlie kept her smile firmly in place, she was suddenly weary of the act. She wanted so badly to say, "Dan, I'm tired of playing the clown. I'm scared of what's happening to us. I'm hurting for you. And more and more every day I'm hurting for me." But she didn't and she wouldn't. He valued her for her ability to make him laugh and she would give him what he needed even if she had to tattoo the smile onto her face.

Gazing out the window at the passing scenery, she forced her mind away from her troubled thoughts and wondered how Mrs. Webster would react to seeing her again. It was not exactly a subject guaranteed to calm her nerves, but it had to be faced sooner or later.

Arlie had met Sarah Webster several weeks after her initial encounter with Dan and even at the tender age of six, had instantly recognized the antagonism in the woman's eyes. At the time she wouldn't admit how much Mrs. Webster's attitude had hurt. She had wanted a mother's love so desperately and after hearing Dan's glowing account of his mother, had woven dreams of a closeness that she knew instantly were hopeless. During the following years she had tried again and again to break down the barriers between them, but her efforts were useless. Mrs. Webster refused to allow her to get close. And Arlie never knew why.

"You're very quiet. Is something wrong?" Dan's voice was soft and concerned as he threw a glance of inquiry at her frowning face.

She shook her head and grinned. "Stage fright. Your mother has never liked me you know," she said wryly. "Are you sure she wanted me to come tonight?"

"Yes, I'm sure," he said firmly. "Her invitation was very specific. She wants us both to be there."

He stared quietly ahead for a moment, then said, "Mom has changed, Arlie. She's more relaxed nowadays. I know there was something wrong between you before, but give her a chance tonight to show you she's different."

"Of course, I'll give her a chance," she said, sliding nearer to him. "I wanted to be close to your mother, but there was always a wall between us. At first, I assumed it was the same thing that kept Daddy from loving me. Then when I discovered his reasons, I figured it was just a personality conflict." She smiled, quietly mocking herself as she said, "Poor unloved Arlie."

"I've always loved you," he said gently.

She drew in a sharp breath, wishing desperately that he meant that in the way she wanted him to mean it. She exhaled slowly and quietly, squeezing his muscular thigh as she said casually, "I know. What do you think keeps me afloat when things get rough? I know I can count on you to be there for me."

He sighed in a curiously pained way, then said in a strange monotone, "Yes, I'll always be there."

Before she could question the lifeless note in his voice, Dan began to ask her about an upcoming student exhibit in which she had been asked to participate. Speaking about the impersonal topic, they covered the distance between Fort Worth and Curry much too quickly for Arlie.

As they pulled into the gravel driveway of the house where she had first encountered Dan, she smiled in reminiscence. The tall flowering shrubs that had been her hiding place still surrounded the house, sending her back to a special time and place.

As they stepped from the car, a weird, yelping howl drew her attention to the side of the house at the same instant a galloping ball of brown fur came flying around the corner.

"Malachai!" she squealed as she and Dan were greeted by the enthusiastic leaps. "You old derelict, I can't believe you're still here." She knelt down to receive a wet kiss from the ragged animal who had turned up on Dan's doorstep in much the same way as Arlie herself. "Lord, you still smell as bad as you always did." She looked up at Dan. "How old is he, for heaven's sake?"

"As near as we can figure, he's twelve," Dan said, pulling her to her feet and calmly picking the clumps of fur from her clothes. "He was about six months old when he found us."

She looked from the homely dog to Dan and murmured softly, "You always end up with the rejects, don't you?" then turned as Dan's brother, Mike, came out to greet them.

He was followed closely by Susie, looking more mature, but just as beautiful as the last time Arlie had seen her. Although Dan's sister had not grown up surrounded by wealth as Arlie had, she had always had serenity, a quiet confidence that Arlie coveted because it came from within. Arlie had bluffed her way through life for so long, the act had become a part of her, but it was still false and covered a deeply ingrained insecurity.

Her reunion with Mike—a younger, less-sober version of Dan—and with Susie was warm and exuberant, the do-you-remember's coming from all participants in a steady stream. Then Arlie was introduced to what seemed like a house full of offspring, who in reality turned out to be two-year-old twin boys for Susie and a giggling three-year-old girl and brand-new son for Mike. Susie's husband and Mike's wife completed the picture and Arlie was complimenting all concerned on the intelligence and wit of their children when Sarah Webster walked into the room.

"Hello, Arlie," Dan's mother said softly, her voice holding a touch of uncertainty.

It had been ten years since Arlie had caught more than a passing glimpse of Mrs. Webster. After Dan moved into a place of his own, Arlie had no reason to come to this house and had in fact avoided the place where she knew she was not welcome. The years had brought definite physical changes to Sarah Webster, but the added wrinkles and gray hair went practically unnoticed by Arlie. The change she was looking for was in the older woman's eyes.

Meeting Arlie's gaze steadily, Mrs. Webster gave her a tentative smile. The sincerity behind the smile startled Arlie and for a moment she couldn't respond. She merely stared at her blankly. Then as she saw doubt cloud the faded hazel eyes and sensed the tension in her stiff stance, Arlie walked toward her swiftly, reaching out to hug her as she had wanted to do so many years before.

"Hello, Mrs. Webster," she murmured.

"Sarah," the older woman corrected, her eyes misting for a moment so briefly, Arlie felt she must have imagined it.

They continued to look at each other, Sarah's eyes silently asking for forgiveness and Arlie's showing that remorse was not necessary, until it hit them simultaneously how quiet the room had become.

Sarah turned to address her family. "Why are you all standing around gaping like a bunch of simpletons? Just go on about your business while Arlie and I put dinner on the table."

Arlie couldn't suppress the giggle that escaped her as they left the room. "Dan sure looked funny with his mouth hanging open, didn't he?"

"Yes, I guess he did at that." Sarah laughed as they walked into the kitchen. "Now, you sit down here," she indicated the small kitchen table, "and I'll fix you a cup of tea."

"I thought we were going to put dinner on the table."

"That can wait. It's time you and I had a talk," Sarah said firmly, then she glanced away uncomfortably, her voice growing less sure. "I can see that you've decided to forgive me for the way I treated you." She stopped Arlie's vehement protest with a raised hand. "There's no getting around it, Arlie. I was cruel. You were just as loving and open then as you are now, but I refused to see it. I wish I could bring back those years and make it up to you, but I can't." She sighed heavily. "What I can do is try and give you an explanation for the way I was then. It's not adequate recompense, but it's all I've got."

Arlie clasped Sarah's small, work-roughened hand in her own. "You don't have to do this, you know. That was yesterday. All that really matters is that we can be friends today."

"You may not need it," Sarah said softly, "but I do. You don't know how many times I've thought of you over the years. Trying to figure out what was wrong with me, why I shut you out like that. Just recently I've met someone, a very wise friend, that I can talk to easily and he's helped me straighten out my thoughts. Now I need to get it out in the open. Therapy of a sort." She shifted in her chair and laughed. "So you see it's really for selfish reasons that I want to explain. May I?"

After Arlie's murmured "Of course," Sarah leaned back in her chair, closed her eyes, and began to speak. "I've never been a very strong woman, Arlie. I was raised in a different time from you. That's not an excuse, just a fact. I depended completely on my husband and when he died, I was lost. It seemed natural to let Dan's strength replace Tom's. Even then, when Dan was only twelve, he was so reliable, so hardworking. He came to me and told me he would take care of us. And, Arlie," Sarah opened her eyes as her voice took on a painfully emphatic note, "he seemed so positive, so strong, that I didn't question his decision. Tom's social security check just wasn't enough to cover everything. I had never had a job so I took in sewing, but Dan wanted Susie and Mike to have more. He wanted them to have the little luxuries that other kids had. So he went to work when he was only twelve. I know other kids work at that age and it wouldn't have been so bad if it had just been the job, but he took over total responsibility for the family. He disciplined and advised his brother and sister just like a father. He tried to take all the worries off my shoulders and carry them on his own."

Arlie could tell that Sarah was approaching a difficult part of her explanation. Her face was pinched with painful memories and her hand trembled as she moved to pour boiling water into their cups. Arlie wanted to make things easier for her, but was helpless to do anything except listen.

"When you came along," Sarah continued, "the pattern was already set. I depended on Dan completely." She drew in an unsteady breath. "As incomprehensible as this sounds, I felt my world, my stability, was being threatened by a six-year-old child. If I had admitted my feelings—if I had even recognized them—I would have seen how ridiculous that was. I'm still not sure of the mental process that brought about my feelings, I just know I was afraid that in some way you would diminish my family's security. I resented the time Dan spent with you. And, I'm ashamed to say, I resented the laughter you brought into his life. I excused myself by saying you were taking away time he should have been spending with his brother and sister. That he had enough to cope with without taking you on, too. But it was all lies. I felt that if he were treating you as one of the family, he was giving away a piece of himself that I wanted for us. It was some sort of twisted survival instinct." Sarah fell silent, staring into her cup as she waited for Arlie's reaction to her fervent rush of words.

But how do I react, Arlie thought helplessly. If she told Sarah how much Dan's care had meant to her, Sarah would feel even guiltier. If she tried to make her believe her attitude had not hurt Arlie, Sarah would know she was lying. Sarah was asking for something from Arlie that she simply didn't know how to give.

"Sarah," she began hesitantly, "everyone has something in their past that they regret, that they're ashamed of. But we can't change the past. All we can do is learn from it. I was a hellion back then and I made my father's life miserable. I regret it, but I can't change it. I can only accept it and go on from there. I don't think you need me to forgive you. I think you need to forgive yourself." Arlie looked up and found Sarah's eyes on her. "If you think about it," Arlie said, giving her a gamine grin, "this would be an awfully dull world if we were all perfect."

"Yes, you're right," Sarah said, her eyes brightening as she shakily returned Arlie's smile. She drew in a deep breath, holding Arlie's hand in a tight clasp that said more than her words. Then she lifted her head in determination and said, "Now I think it's time we put that dinner on the table."

"One thing first," Arlie said as they both stood.

"You said something about a friend—a male friend. Is it serious?"

Sarah ran a hand over her thick salt and pepper hair, avoiding Arlie's eyes as she answered. "Yes, I guess it is."

"Sarah," she teased. "You're blushing. I wish I could do that. It makes you look so pretty. My face goes all splotchy when I lose my temper, but I never blush. You look just like a Jane Austin heroine."

"Stop teasing me," she pleaded in an urgent whisper. "I don't know what I'm going to tell the kids. They don't even know about Frank and he wants me to marry him." She looked at Arlie, panic showing in her face. "How am I going to tell them?"

Arlie put her arm around the older woman and gave her a squeeze. "It's very simple. You just tell them you have to get married because you're pregnant. That'll shake them up."

"Arlie!" she gasped, her face turning bright red. Then laughter burst from her, shaking her small body until she leaned against the counter weakly.

"What's going on?" Dan stood in the open doorway, trying to look stern, but his eyes showed his pleasure at the sight of the two laughing women. He walked into the room, folding his arms as he scolded, "Have you two been into the cooking sherry? I thought you came out here to get dinner together."

"Dan," Sarah gasped. "How on earth have you managed to put up with her for so many years? She's terrible."

"Well, well," he said, chuckling. "A corroborating witness. I've always told Arlie she would try the patience of a saint and I guess you're as close to a saint as I'm going to get."

"Very funny," Arlie said. "If you two are going to

gang up on me, I'll just take myself elsewhere." She picked up a large platter of chicken and walked to the door, pausing to glance back over her shoulder. "By the way, Dan, I believe Sarah has something she wants to tell you."

As she left the room followed by Dan's puzzled look and Sarah's panicky gasp, she wondered if Dan's mother would thank her for forcing the issue. But she knew that she could count on Dan to provide his mother with the support she needed now. When she walked back into the kitchen, Sarah was being swallowed by Dan's enthusiastic bear-hug and Arlie didn't regret her interference in the least.

At dinner Sarah told the rest of the family about her engagement and, after a tense moment when everyone seemed to be in shock, they all responded as enthusiastically as Arlie could have wished. Throughout the rest of the meal, Sarah was subjected to a lot of good-natured teasing about her beau, but she held up like a trooper, her still-beautiful face beaming with relief and happiness.

At first, Arlie sat quietly, enjoying the camaraderie of the relaxed family atmosphere, but she was quickly drawn into the cheerfully noisy banter. And she loved every minute of it. Especially the small things. Things like helping Mike's daughter, Shannon, secretly remove the bits of onion from her potato salad. Or helping the twins finish off their green beans so they could have their dessert. These were the things that Arlie treasured for it meant she was accepted by the family she had always coveted. Although it was not the first time she had been included in a family dinner, she had never before felt as though she were a part of the family. It was a strange and heady experience, one she was reluctant to have end.

But like all good things, end it did. And all too

soon she and Dan were standing on the porch, fielding the fat June bugs that were bent on dive-bombing the light as they said their good-byes. It helped to know that they left with an invitation to come back soon and meet Sarah's Frank.

She glanced over her shoulder and watched as the waving group on the porch grew smaller and finally disappeared when the white Lincoln turned the corner to pull out onto the highway leading back to Fort Worth. The evening had been so wonderful, so real, that Arlie had to wrestle with herself to keep from slipping back into her childhood practice of pretending—pretending Dan's family was hers.

"You're sitting too far away." Dan's voice was low and husky as though he were afraid of disturbing the soft, velvet darkness of the country night. When she slid across the seat, he put his arm around her shoulder, drawing her closer. "You enjoyed tonight, didn't you, sweet?" he murmured quietly.

"It was the loveliest evening I've had in a long time, Dan. I envy you and your family."

Slowing the car, he pulled off the highway into a small, tree-canopied roadside park. He reached over to kill the engine, then shifted sideways to lean with his back against the door, pulling her along with him. The sounds of the night filled the car as he released her ponytail, spreading the long, silky hair around her shoulders, then he lifted a lock to rub it softly against his lips. When he caught the question in her eyes, he traced the outline of her lips with one long finger and said slowly, "Have you ever thought about having your own family?"

For a moment Arlie thought he was talking about her covetous daydreams concerning his family and she stared at him blankly, then she realized he meant children of her own. "It's something I don't let myself think about too often," she said softly, shivering as he slid his hand under her hair to caress her neck. "Somehow it doesn't seem possible for me. I know this sounds silly, but a family . . . children . . . I've always been afraid to think of it because I want it so badly." She gave a small, hesitant laugh. "Like not telling a wish because then it won't come true."

"You'd be a good mother," he murmured. "I watched you with Susie's and Mike's kids. They love you because you treat them like people . . . you don't talk down to them." With a large hand on the back of her neck, he drew her head down to his chest, making it impossible for her to see his face. "Why don't we get married, Arlie?"

The words seemed to fill the night, reverberating crazily in her brain. She closed her eyes, squeezing them tightly shut as she felt her heart miss a beat. She drew in a shaky breath, expelling it slowly and painfully. "You're insane, aren't you?" She laughed unsteadily. "Wouldn't we just make a great couple? The devil and Daniel Webster . . . remember?"

" 'And the devil hath the power to assume a pleasing shape,' " he quoted softly. "You please me, Arlie."

"But I make you crazy," she objected, pulling back to stare at him, refusing to give in to the dizzying warmth that threatened to overwhelm her. "You know I do."

"Well, there is that," he admitted, chuckling softly. "But you made me crazy with worry when you were married to Stephan. You have to marry some day—for real—then I'll go through all the worry again. This way I would know that you were being taken care of." He picked up her hand, turning it palm up as he lifted it to his lips, then sighed and held it to his cheek and continued. "I know I've been acting strange lately, but it's from the nature of our situation. It's like being in limbo. I've never been able to handle temporary relationships. They make me nervous. I want something solid . . . something I can count on. If we were married, I could settle down and stop worrying about it."

"You mean like a cartoon you've finished working on," she asked skeptically. "You file it away and forget about it."

"I'm handling this badly, aren't I?" he said wryly. "I simply wanted you to know that I wouldn't continue to have my weird moods if we get married. I think we have something special." Sliding his hand under her skirt, he smoothed the warm flesh before letting it come to rest on the softness of her inner thigh. "You said you had never been physically attracted to anyone else. I know that's not enough to base a lifetime relationship on, but it's a good starting point. We know each other better than most people do after they've been married for years. You're the only woman I've ever wanted to have children with and . . ." he looked away, out into the dark night, ". . . we love each other. Maybe not in the accepted way," he added when he heard her muffled gasp, "but it's a good, solid thing and it's more than most people ever have."

Arlie swallowed a solid lump of pain in her throat, overlooking the last of his reasons to latch onto something less hurtful. "We could have babies? Soon?"

His hand on her thigh tightened suddenly. "Wouldn't . . ." His voice came out harsh and raspy. He shook his head and cleared his throat to begin again. "Wouldn't you want to finish college first?"

"I would have nine months to learn the basics

of photography," she said, a light kindling in her dark eyes as the idea began to take hold. She threw her arms around his neck, hugging him tightly as she rained kisses on his face. "Dan . . . a baby!" She drew back abruptly. "When? When can we start?"

"Slow down," he laughed. "We'd better get married first." His face suddenly grew serious. "And before we do that I want you to take some time to think about it. I don't want to rush you into anything. I want you to be sure before we go any further."

"But I don't need to think about it," she protested.

"Yes, you do. You're too impulsive and this is much too serious to be treated as a whim."

Arlie stared up at him, frowning when she saw the firm conviction in his face. She bit her lower lip and began to play with the top button of his plaid shirt. "Dan," she said, her voice sweetly cajoling. "We don't really have to wait, do we?"

"Yes, we do."

Undeterred by the determination in his voice, she slipped the button loose and slid her hand inside his shirt, moving it sensuously over the rough hairs on his chest. "If you think that's best, then of course that's what we'll do," she said innocently, releasing the rest of the buttons to move her lips across the area her hand had already explored.

"You're not fooling anyone, you demon," he said hoarsely as his heartbeat quickened under her hand. "You think you'll seduce me into changing my mind and you're wrong."

She slid her hand beneath his belt buckle, then as he drew in a deep breath, moved it lower. "Do you want me to stop?"

"God, no," he gasped, shifting his long legs to

accomodate her body as he grasped her buttocks and pulled her close.

Her skirt slid up around her waist with the movement and she felt his hard male strength as he pressed her urgently close. When a groan began deep in his chest and he dipped his head to assuage the need that burned in them both, Arlie was ready, meeting his hungry mouth in an explosive kiss. She moved her hands beneath his shirt to massage the firm muscles of his back, the fire inside her growing with each kneading caress.

"You really are a devil," he groaned. "I haven't made love in a car since I was eighteen and I'm not about to renew the practice at this point in my life."

But his words didn't match his actions for as he spoke he was unbuttoning her blouse. He spread warm, moist kisses down her throat to the rounded tops of her heaving breasts, urgently pressing the rounded flesh to his lips, capturing the hard nipples gently between his teeth as he heard her moaning response. He shifted his body again, intending to draw her beneath him, only to stop abruptly, swearing softly as the steering wheel cut into his ribs. He drew himself up, lifting her to the seat beside him.

"Move over," he said running a shaking hand through his hair. When she slid over a couple of inches, he motioned with his hand. "All the way over . . . against the door."

"If I move over any farther, I'll be out the door," she complained as she did up her blouse.

"Which would probably be a very good thing," he muttered darkly. "Now, as soon as I calm down enough to drive we'll go home."

She looked at him in the shadow filled car. "Are you mad at me?"

"Yes." His voice was short and uncompromising.

"Because I was trying to make you change your mind?"

"Because you make me lose control . . . and in the dumbest places. God! Making love in a car." His voice was rich with disgust for himself.

"You can huff and puff all you want, Daniel Webster, but I for one enjoyed myself thoroughly." She looked over at him as he started the engine and pulled back onto the highway. "Who?" she asked suddenly.

"Who what?" he returned, his voice distracted.

"Who did you make love to in a car when you were eighteen? I bet it was that fat, blonde cheerleader. What was her name? It sounded like a sneeze . . . I always wanted to say 'God bless you' when you mentioned her name."

"Her name was Anna Sue and she wasn't fat. She was . . . voluptuous."

"Is that why you made love to her in a car, because she was fa . . . voluptuous?"

She watched as he tightened his lips to keep them from twitching in amusement. "I didn't say I made love to her at all. You said that."

"But you didn't deny it. Why could you make love to her in a car but not me?"

"Arlie," he said in exasperation. "We have a lovely bed at home that fits my size much better. When I was eighteen I had no choice. Now I do, but if it will make you happy, we'll stop right now and I'll just have to hang my feet out the window."

She felt the laughter bubbling up inside her until it overflowed and the soft, infectious sound filled the car. "I'm almost tempted," she chuckled. "If only to see your feet hanging out the window."

"You would be," he said wryly, sharing her laughter. "Come here, pest."

"I thought I was banished to Siberia?" she said, lifting an inquiring eyebrow.

"Are you going to waste time pointing out that I have no willpower where you're concerned or are you going to get over here and fill this empty space?" he asked drily, giving her no chance to answer as he reached out to pull her close.

Fill the empty space, she thought, sobering suddenly. Could she do that for him? Dan had told her to think over his proposal and make sure it was right for her. Arlie knew without a doubt what was right for her, but the question was— what was right for Dan?

Nine

It was a question that was to stay with her constantly in the days to follow. Dan was a grown man, she would argue silently. He should know his own mind better than anyone else. But he was also a man who was in the habit of forgetting his own needs in favor of other's, she would counter. If he thought it was right for Arlie, he wouldn't even stop to wonder whether or not it was right for him. But I'll be a good wife for him, she pleaded with her silent adversary. I'll be sober and trustworthy and conventional. I'll even make the ultimate sacrifice—I'll be on time.

All those things couldn't change the fact that being a good wife had nothing to do with being the *right* wife and no matter how she argued with herself, she couldn't get past the fact that Dan didn't love her in the special way he should love a woman he was going to spend the rest of his life with. Was it fair knowingly to let him rob himself of that kind of relationship?

Through all her mental battles Dan offered no help at all. His strange mood swings ceased abruptly after the night of his proposal as though, having taken action, the problem no longer cut into his peace. He didn't try to influence her in any way. He didn't push her for a decision. He simply waited.

To further confuse her, he no longer avoided people. They had seen more people in the few days after their visit to Curry than they had in the whole month that went before it. And tonight they were coming out of isolation with a vengeance, for Dan had invited twenty of his friends and business associates to an outdoor barbeque. Although Arlie was accustomed to entertaining and the thought of playing hostess held no terrors for her, she was flabbergasted by his sudden about-face.

She dressed with particular care for the evening, donning a vivid red, strapless jumpsuit with wide flowing legs, and left her hair loose, pinning it back on one side with a gold barrette. Her long, flowing ebony locks gave her the sensuous look of a sophisticated gypsy.

As she stood in the kitchen preparing the salad and wrapping potatoes in aluminum foil, she couldn't shake the feeling that tonight would be important in some way. Perhaps the feeling came from the sparkle of anticipation she saw in Dan's eyes. Whatever the cause, perhaps tonight would bring answers to the questions that had been plaguing her.

Suddenly Arlie found herself surrounded by strong arms and the equally strong odor of charcoal lighter fluid. As she turned to confront her attacker, she said, "What have you been doing—bathing in that stuff? You smell . . ." She stopped abruptly as she took in his appearance. "Daniel Webster! You get away from me this minute. Look at yourself," she scolded, indicating the black smears on his gray sleeveless sweatshirt and the ragged cut-offs that reached down to mid-thigh. "You look like an oversized chimney sweep."

"I couldn't stop myself," he said, grinning. "It was an irresistible impulse. I'll bet if you polled a hundred men, the majority would say that upon finding a sexy gypsy in their kitchens their first impulse would be to throw her on the floor and ravish her."

"Huh!" she snorted inelegantly. "You don't really think that would hold up in court, do you? Now hurry up and get changed before your guests arrive and catch you dressed like a filthy ragpicker."

"I knew it," he said sadly. "You only love me for my sartorial elegance."

"Dan," she said impatiently, glancing at the wall clock.

"I'm going already." He started to leave, but turned to look at her as he reached the door. "Did I ever tell you that when you're mad your eyes turn deep purple . . . like African violets?" Just as she opened her mouth to scream in frustration, he added softly, "They turn that color when I make love to you, too."

Arlie felt fire ripple through her as his words conjured up vivid pictures of their bodies pressed together in passion. She leaned against the counter weakly and looked up to find him gone. Damn him! Just when she thought she could predict his every action, he would do something to disconcert her completely. There was a gleam of suppressed excitement in his eyes tonight that left her unsettled. She felt a sudden, unexplainable insecurity and wished they could cancel the party until their future plans were more certain.

But thirty minutes later when they opened the door to the first arrivals, she had put the feeling aside to play hostess. Arlie enjoyed entertaining and threw herself into her role with vivacious enthusiasm and contagious warmth. Although to her their guests were practically strangers, they were still subject to the same foibles and frailties as people the world over. So she circulated, stimulating conversation and breaking up cliques, too busy to notice the raised eyebrows, the whispers concealed behind raised hands.

When Eric and Diane arrived, minutes after the elder Prescotts, it suddenly occurred to Arlie that she hadn't seen Eric since his parents' party—the first night she had made love to Dan. Although Diane had dropped by unannounced on several occasions, Eric had not once accompanied her.

Later as she laughingly turned away from a barrage of overdone flattery thrown at her by a distinguished newspaper executive, she found herself face to face with a frowning Eric.

"Can I talk to you for a minute?" he asked quietly.

"Of course," she replied, puzzled by his serious expression. "Come to the kitchen with me. We're running low on gin and ice." She led the way to the kitchen, unaware of the speculative looks that followed them.

Once in the kitchen Eric wasted no time. "Arlie, what's going on?" he asked as the door swung shut behind them. "I've called and called and Dan keeps putting me off with stupid excuses." He turned away from her abruptly. "Look, I know I got out of line the last time I saw you. The fact that I had too much to drink is not much of an excuse, but even if I were stone cold sober . . ."

well, I thought we were friends. Did I offend you so deeply that you can't bring yourself to speak to me?"

"Eric!" she said in surprise. "Of course you didn't." Why hadn't Dan told her of Eric's calls? "I'm sorry you were worried. If I had known what you were thinking, I would have gotten in touch with you." She laughed wryly. "The truth is I've been so busy—I'm taking some courses at the community college—everything else has gone out of my head. But honestly, Eric . . ." she placed her hand on his shoulder and he turned to face her, ". . . I haven't given it another thought." She looked at him with a mischievous gleam in her eyes, her lips curling in a grin. "And besides, I think you were more perturbed that night than I was."

"You've got that right," he admitted ruefully. "You scared the hell out of me. It was the most effective means of self-defense I've ever seen. A karate chop wouldn't have sobered me half as quickly."

"They don't call me Killer for nothing!" She chuckled as she turned and walked to the refrigerator. "Now take this in to the mob before they become vicious." She shoved a bucket of ice into his arms and followed him out the door, carrying two bottles to restock the liquor supply.

Arlie was laughing at one of Eric's irreverent comments when they entered the living room seconds later and it was a moment before she noticed the peculiar silence that hung over the room. She looked around in curiosity before throwing a questioning look at an unexplainably red-faced Eric, then as the conversation picked up, she shrugged mentally and began to circulate again.

Later as they ate the delicious steaks Dan had broiled on the grill, Arlie and Diane sat in a quiet corner of the backyard, gossiping leisurely. After watching Diane tonight, Arlie's admiration for the older woman had grown, but she found that her admiration was tinged with something new—envy. Diane was not only beautiful—she belonged. Standing at Dan's side, Diane had joined in the political and business discussions with an ease and intelligence that made Arlie feel slightly inadequate. She found herself thinking what a good wife Diane would make for Dan. But before that self-destructive line of thought could take hold, Arlie had shaken herself out of imminent self-pity and begun to regain her self-confidence. Even though she didn't possess the knowledge that Diane did, she would some day. Arlie knew she was intelligent enough to master any subject, given the right incentives. And Dan was incentive enough for any woman. Arlie would be the kind of wife he needed . . . eventually.

She came out of her reverie when she felt a strange prickle on the back of her neck. Turning, she glanced around the yard to find the cause. Near the patio door, a tall, gray-haired man was staring at her intently. This was not the first time tonight she had caught him staring and she found there was something in his look that made her vaguely uncomfortable.

"Diane," she whispered. "Who is that man over by the door . . . the one in the blue shirt? I know Dan introduced him to me, but I can't remember."

Diane turned to look over her shoulder, then turned back to Arlie. "That's Marshall Simon. He's editor for one of the Phoenix papers that picked up Dan's cartoon strip. He looks a little green around the gills, doesn't he?" She took another bite of steak, then looked thoughtfully at Dan as she said, "After his cartoon makes its debut next month, Dan's going to find himself dealing with more and more men like Mr. Simon.

I'm so excited for him. His political cartoons were popular, but he's moving into a whole new realm now. He's going to be famous," Diane said with quiet conviction.

Arlie felt pride well up inside her. She believed Diane. And she believed in Dan's ability. Glancing again over her shoulder, she found the mysterious Mr. Simon was no longer in evidence and wondered if the strange stares were caused by her reputation. Surely after she and Dan were married the speculation and gossip would die down. People usually got caught up in the news of the moment, forgetting what happened yesterday.

As she let her eyes drift over the small crowd, she was stopped by a sight that caused her eyes to narrow in displeasure. An unfamiliar but very sexy auburn-haired woman was doing her best to rub the skin off one of Dan's bare arms with scarlet-tipped caressing fingers.

"And who is *that*?" she asked, turning back to Diane. "I know Dan didn't introduce me to her. I would have remembered her."

Diane laughed. "That, my dear, is our adorable Sheila. She writes a regular column for the magazine and has been after Dan since she first laid eyes on him." She shook her head. "Someone really ought to tell her that she hasn't a prayer."

"Oh?" Arlie said skeptically, her voice tinged with jealousy. "It looks to me like she's making definite progress. Look at Dan grinning at her like a big, dumb fool."

"I'm not saying she couldn't get into his bed," Diane admitted. "After all, Dan's human and she does have a certain . . . something. But Sheila's after marriage and Dan will never marry someone like her."

"What's wrong with her?" Since Arlie was caught in a hammerlock by the green-eyed monster she could naturally see dozens of things wrong with the voluptuous redhead, but she was eager to have Diane give her logical reasons to dislike the woman.

"Sheila is a legend in her own way. A very small, very sad legend, but a legend nonetheless," Diane said quietly, her voice holding something close to compassion. "She is probably hated by more wives in the publishing industry than anyone else you could name. That's why I know Dan would never have anything to do with her. He's much too fastidious. Affairs are one thing, indiscriminate bed-hopping is something else entirely. And besides . . ." Diane smiled, ". . . if he did decide to marry someone like that, I'd stop him myself. He's too good a friend and he has worked too hard building his career. I couldn't see him jeopardize it without doing something to prevent it."

"A bad marriage could do that?" Arlie felt a sharp pain in her chest as she saw the parallel between herself and Sheila. Could her reputation harm Dan's career?

"Oh yes, it very definitely could." It took a moment of shock for Arlie to realize Diane was answering her spoken question, not her silent one. "You and I see Dan as a strong, quiet, conventional sort of man," Diane continued, "but believe me not everyone sees him in that light. He has a reputation as a rebel—a troublemaker—in some quarters and he's made some pretty powerful enemies through his cartoons. In fact, there are newspapers in this supposedly democratic country that are not allowed to run Dan's material. Things are beginning to calm down, thank God, and this new strip will put him back on top. But just one wrong move and he'll be back where he started. They would use anything to discredit him," Diane said vehemently. "Can you imagine what ammunition they would have if Dan were involved with Sheila who has such a sordid reputation?"

"You mean they would blackmail him?" Arlie glanced surreptitiously at the woman sitting beside her. Had Dan told Diane he had proposed to her? Somehow she didn't think so. Although she might feel just as strongly about Arlie as she obviously did about Sheila, Diane did not strike her as a devious person.

"I don't know how they would use the information. I simply know they would. And it could only cause more trouble for Dan."

Arlie looked around the patio, suddenly feeling a frantic need to see Dan, to ask him about the depressing possibilities Diane had raised. But now he was nowhere in sight. She excused herself to her companion and made her way through the mingling guests, each of whom seemed determined to detain her.

After checking the kitchen, Arlie walked toward Dan's study and was reaching out to push open the door that stood slightly ajar when raised voices in the room stopped her.

"I'm sorry, Dan," Eric said. "I wasn't trying to make a scene, but I couldn't let him get away with what he was saying about Arlie."

"I said nothing but the truth," answered a voice that Arlie couldn't identify. There was a disturbing, almost rabid, quality about the tense, slurred voice. "I called her a slut and that's what she is. It makes me sick to my stomach to see her flitting around looking like a pretty butterfly, knowing all the time that like the butterfly, she feeds on carrion. She's filth . . . beautiful filth . . . and you two can't see it because you're both bedding her."

Arlie leaned weakly against the wall as she heard a high, demented sound that was frighteningly like a laugh, then the scuffle of feet and Eric's rasped, "You bastard!" followed quickly by Dan's quiet, "That's enough, Eric. You can't fight Arlie's reputation. You would spend your whole life fighting if you tried."

Oh God! she moaned silently, the blood draining from her face. She had wanted tonight to bring answers, but she hadn't expected to be crucified by them. She closed her eyes as the pain began exploding in her chest, tightening her throat with its strangling power. She wanted to run, to hide under a dark porch as she had done when she was ten.

But, in the grip of a nightmarish paralysis, her limbs refused to move and she could only lean against the wall and let the terrible words lash her.

"Yes, Eric," the raspy, unfamiliar voice sneered. "You listen to him. He knows that I'm only repeating what everyone has been saying all evening. You think we didn't know what you were doing out in the kitchen? You should thank me for warning you . . . you've got time . . . no, don't turn away from me, I'm trying to help you . . ." The man's voice took on a high, almost hysterical note. "Don't let her . . . don't let her . . ."

"Marshall!" Dan's voice was low and firm. "You're not feeling well. Why don't you let me take you home."

Arlie flinched as Dan was answered by the man's eerie laugh, then more scuffling sounds before the man continued. "No! Get your hands off me. Always so calm . . . so sure of yourself. You think because you've hidden her away people are going to forget what she's like. But I've got news for you, Mr. Hotshot Cartoonist. We didn't forget and we won't. You've made a lot of enemies and I'm going to laugh myself sick when they destroy your little world."

Arlie no longer felt the pain that had wrenched her body moments before. She felt only a terrible numbness as though her soul had hidden away from hurt. Opening her eyes, she began to walk back toward the living room, her steps faltering as a couple stepped out into the hall.

She took a deep breath and continued toward them, a bright smile appearing effortlessly on her emotionless face. "You're not leaving so soon? I apologize for deserting you, but I was trying to track down our elusive host. If you'll wait here, I'll drag him out of hiding." She leaned toward the smiling middle-aged woman and asked ruefully, "Why can't men stop working long enough to enjoy themselves?"

The older woman chuckled. "Well, Arlie, if Dan is anything like my Sam, work is the only thing he really enjoys."

"Now, Mother," her husband replied. "I wouldn't say that. How do you think we got six kids?"

"Sam!" the older woman gasped, then joined her husband and Arlie in laughter.

She murmured a hurried excuse to the friendly couple, then, turning away, felt an involuntary aftershock of pain cross her face as she called loudly, "Dan, where are you?" forcing herself to sound confident. She walked back to the studio, calling his name again before she drew in a deep breath, arranged her face, and pushed the door open.

"So this is where you're hiding away," she said as she walked into the room. "Why are the three best looking men in the house holing up in here?" She looked around the room, her face never losing its artificial gaity as the tense silence hit her like a blast of cold air. She recognized the man now. He was the same man who had been staring at her all evening. The one Diane had identified as Marshall Simon. She also recognized the expressions on the other two men's faces before they managed to mask them. Eric's contained the frustrated anger she had heard in his voice. But it was Dan's that caused the bile to rise in her throat. For in Dan's face was embarrassment and shame.

She walked to stand beside Dan, looking at the other two men with a smile as she said, "Now, you both can just go back and join the party while Dan plays host and says goodnight to two of his guests." She took Dan's hand, forcing herself not to flinch as his grip tightened on her fingers. She led him out into the hall. "Mr. and Mrs. Ames are ready to leave," she murmured, then lifted his hand triumphantly as she saw the couple watching their approach. "Just like the Mounties," she said. "I always get my man."

The blessed numbness held through Dan's apologies to the couple, helping her to find the appropriate phrases as they took their leave. It held through the remainder of the party and it held when she entertained the stragglers who seemed determined to spend the night. It even held when Diane insisted on staying to help Arlie and Dan stack things for the cleaning lady and then began to discuss an upcoming theme issue of her father's magazine with Dan. It held as she said goodnight and walked to her old bedroom. But as she closed the door behind her, it left her completely, deserting her with a debilitating swiftness, draining her of all her strength. She slumped to the floor, feeling the weight of the truth press her lower.

So many things were explained now. The way Dan had isolated her from his friends. His erratic mood swings. He had been afraid of his friends' reactions to her reputation. Maybe tonight had been some kind of test. Perhaps he had wanted to see if people could forget and accept her as his wife.

She began to laugh . . . silently, feverishly . . . beating her fists against the cushioning carpet. He should have known better. She should have known better. The vicious bastards would never forget. The vultures would continue to circle, waiting eagerly for their victim to finally give up. They were small-minded busybodies and they had ruined everything. They had . . .

No. That was wrong. They hadn't ruined anything. She looked down at her hands, unclenching them slowly to reveal the smears of blood left behind when her fingernails had pierced her palms. It suddenly seemed funny—hysterically funny—that she felt no pain, only the warmth of her own blood. Just as she was responsible for mutilating her hands, so was she solely responsible for mutilating her life.

" 'We have met the enemy and they is us,' " she misquoted aloud, giggling suddenly as the sound of her own voice startled her.

Everything had been a great damn joke to her. She had actually enjoyed fooling all her so-called friends into thinking she was as bad or worse than they. She had mistakenly thought she was punishing them for their silliness, never giving a thought to the fact that she was also fooling the sane, decent people who read about her. And so, in the end, she had succeeded only in punishing herself. And Dan for caring about her.

Dan. The shame she had seen in his eyes impaled her now, jerking her to her feet. She couldn't leave the responsibility of ending it to him. She had to do it herself. He would be hurt when she left, but in some secret corner of his mind, wouldn't there also be relief? The fact that he had hidden her away from his friends made it plain that he had anticipated their feelings toward her, even before this evening's fiasco.

She accepted the reasons behind his actions. She even told herself that his reaction to the scene tonight was normal—anyone would have reacted in the same way . . . felt the same embarrassment . . . but some hidden part of her that she wouldn't allow to the surface was dying from the pain of his desertion.

She walked to the window, pulling the curtain aside to stare out into the night. She didn't see the brilliance of the stars, the fullness of the moon. She saw only the engulfing darkness. Biting her lip to hold back a groan, she recalled his words on the night they first made love. "Nothing can destroy our friendship, Arlie," he had said. And he was right. It hadn't been destroyed, but it had been hopelessly crippled. Even if Dan still wanted to marry her, she had no wish to live with guilt as her constant companion.

Frantically, she began making plans for her future. She would move away, away from Fort Worth, maybe even away from Texas. If she began using her maiden name and lived a quiet life, surely then she could have some peace. Surely she could then escape the past. But how could there be peace without Dan? How could she ever escape loving him?

The pressure in her chest grew unbearable and her eyes burned feverishly as she faced the tormenting image of perpetual emptiness. Why can't I cry! she screamed silently. Why can't I have at least that small measure of relief?

Jerking in surprise, she looked down and saw that the curtain now lay at her feet, the window stripped as bare as her emotions. She lifted the crisp fabric to her face, cooling her burning skin, trying to hide from the crucifying thoughts. She needed Dan. She needed him to soothe the hurt and make everything all right. She needed him to protect her from the pain of loving him.

But this time she was on her own. If she told him, he would insist on marrying her and that would destroy them both. This time she had to be strong enough to handle it herself. Now was the time to prove she was his friend. She had to keep him from making a terrible mistake . . . it was time to remove the albatross from around his neck.

Suddenly she heard his footsteps, slow and steady on the stairs. Dropping the curtain, she smoothed back her hair with distraught, jerky motions and moved toward the door as she heard him call her name. Before she could reach the door, it opened and Dan walked in.

"Why are you in here in the dark?" he asked gently, then before she could stop him, he switched on the light, momentarily blinding her.

She blinked, allowing her pupils to adjust, then watched his face as he glanced from the curtain lying on the floor to her. His gaze lingered on her mouth and she reached up to touch it, her eyes widening in surprise as she felt her swollen lower lip. She smiled, hesitantly at first, then with more strength as she slipped into her role. "I should have stopped after two glasses of wine," she laughed, indicating the curtain. "I seem to be a little wobbly on my feet."

"Arlie . . ." he began, his voice filled with concern, his sharp brown eyes never leaving her face.

She whirled around, unable to bear his questioning gaze. "Dan," she interrupted him urgently, "let's go to bed." Her mask slipped with the last word, allowing her voice to break, giving the request a desperate, pleading quality. She shuddered, trying to pull herself together, then felt his arms come around her and she slumped against him as he lifted her to carry her into their bedroom.

His steps never slowing, he walked straight to the bed, leaning over her as he lay her on it. Silently he pulled the silky, red fabric down to her waist and moved his mouth to her breast with voracious hunger, seeming to sense that she needed a fierce loving tonight.

Framing his face with her hands, she pressed his face deeper into her burning flesh, groaning wildly as he sucked and bit and massaged her aching breasts. His lips never left her skin as his hands urgently unfastened the wide belt at her waist and slid the jumpsuit down her body.

She was on fire for him. This would be the last time he held her, the last time he brought her this ferocious pleasure. She wanted the feel of his lips, his hands, indelibly imprinted on her body. This time would have to last forever.

As she began to peel off her hose and panties, his hands went to the buttons of his shirt. "No," she breathed. "Let me . . . please."

He dropped his hands and watched her silently as she swiftly unfastened the buttons, then spread his shirt. She brought her hands up across his chest, threading her fingers in the thick mat of hair, then over his shoulders under his shirt to slide it off. Rising to her knees, she let her hands continue down his back and buried her face in the curve of his neck. She explored his breastbone with her lips and her tongue, savoring the taste and texture of his warm flesh.

When her exploration took her to the hard male nipples, he groaned deep in his chest and yanked her head up to seek her mouth. At the last moment, he remembered her tender lip and gripped her chin, forcing her lips apart so that his tongue could enter the sweet depths without touching the injured flesh. But the caress was so incredibly erotic, she couldn't stand even the minute distance between them and pressed against his mouth urgently, feeling no pain, just incredible pleasure.

Sliding her hands from his shoulders to his waist, she grappled with the buckle, feeling a sudden sense of freedom when it gave way to her fumbling fingers. He moved away and moments later was pushing her roughly back to the bed to fall heavily across her, his breath coming in short, hoarse gasps that echoed her own. She felt his pulsing male strength press into her, his hand sliding down to spread her thighs.

When he entered her with a quick, hard thrust she met him hungrily, pulling him into her fiercely, spurring him on in their frenzied mating. Arlie gave herself completely, unable to hold back one iota of the love that was in her, and the volcanic conclusion that sent her mind into uncaring bliss, freed her for the moment from torment.

But only for a moment, for while she still lingered in the hazy fog of pleasure, Dan moved to turn on the light, then said quietly, "Now, do you want to tell me what's going on?"

Ten

Arlie pulled the sheet over her head as the bright light began to dissipate her beautiful dream. She wasn't ready for it to end. She wasn't ready for reality to steal away the warmth. She wasn't ready, but she didn't fight him when he gently pulled the sheet from her clutching fingers.

"Open your eyes, Arlie." His voice was quiet, yet firm and when she raised her reluctant lids, he repeated softly, "What's going on?" He touched her swollen lip with one gentle finger, then raised her palms to kiss each in turn. "What's bothering you, babe?"

The loving concern in his voice threatened to swamp her and she rose abruptly, walking to the closet to pull out her robe. She looked down as she tied the belt, avoiding his eyes. "This is going to be a toughie, Dan," she said, her voice wry, but steady. "I don't know how to start." She looked down at her clammy hands. "Lord, I wish I smoked. I can't understand how I missed out on that vice." She sucked in her breath. "You were right to make me take time to think over your proposal. I wanted a family of my own so badly . . . I didn't stop to consider how wrong the whole thing was."

She waited in anxious silence for his reaction and when it didn't come, she lifted her eyes to examine his face, but found no clue there. No quickly disguised relief. No regret, no anger. His expression was unreadable as he simply sat and stared at her. She grimaced and continued to speak. "I think I'll get a place of my own, Dan. You know, I've never been truly on my own. I want to make friends that are my own. Not Daddy's or Stephan's or yours." Arlie swallowed nervously as his silence continued. "And something else I've been thinking about . . . you said I had never been physically attracted to anyone else—and of course you're right—but I was a virgin then. Now that I'm not, I could very well find that I'm attracted to all kinds of men." Her voice took on a feverish note as she mentally begged him to accept her excuse. "It's certainly something we should consider. I mean . . . marriage is a lifetime thing. I really shouldn't go into it until I'm sure. It would be terrible if we got married and then I found out that I was turned on by anything in pants." She laughed in agitation. "And it sure would be an uncomfortable position for you to be in."

Pausing to catch her breath, she gave him an exasperated look as he sat, calm and quiet. "Well, say something, damn it. Do you agree or disagree or am I boring you stiff?"

He held her gaze, staring at her steadily until she looked away in discomfort. "You're lying," he said, his voice soft and sure. "Why?"

Moaning, she turned away to pace in frustration. "Look, I didn't want to hurt your feelings. Why can't you just accept what I'm saying? Why do you have to probe?" Stopping abruptly, she turned to face him in desperation. "It's boring here. Your friends are boring. Your life is boring. I'm stagnating here."

"Why are you lying to me?" he repeated in a quiet, stubborn voice.

She pulled her fingers through her long hair, tightening them in the strands, welcoming the twinges of pain. Walking to the bed, she sat down beside him. "Dan, listen to me. We're friends. The best and truest friends in the world. But still just friends. We would be cheating each other if we tried to pretend we were anything more." She picked up one of his large hands and held it between both of hers. "You're such a special person. You deserve a special kind of love . . . and selfishly, I want that special kind of love, too. I want . . . I *need* someone to love me in that special way."

He looked down at their entwined fingers. "And what way is that?"

Sighing, she closed her eyes. "I want a man whose love for me goes all the way to the heart of him. Someone who has a special need—an emptiness in his soul—that only I, Arlie Hunicutt Fleming, can fill." She opened her eyes and shrugged helplessly. "Someone who will love me with as much depth and fullness when I'm ninety as when I'm twenty-six. A man who allows me to be more than Arlie, the clown. Who knows that I hurt, even though I can't cry . . . that I'm afraid, even when I'm pretending to be fearless . . . and when I laugh louder and longer than anyone else, that I'm fighting loneliness and insecurity in the only way I know. I want someone who sees me as I am—with all my faults—and loves me anyway, because that's what makes me . . . me."

He stared at her silently for a moment, then looked down at the floor. "I love you like that, Arlie," he said quietly.

The room swam dizzily in front of her eyes and his next words barely penetrated the fog that cushioned her shock.

"I love you as a friend, as a lover, as a woman . . . as a human being," came the soft, incredible words. "I love you so much that it scares me sometimes . . . it's terrifyingly close to obsession and I don't want that for you." He paused, breathing deeply. "You've never been able to hide your fear or loneliness or pain from me. I see beneath the mask and I love the sensitivity it tries to disguise. Your courage, your intelligence, your humanity . . . they're all a part of you. Just as much as what you call your faults. I see you as you are and I love what I see."

"You can't," she whispered, her eyes opened wide in fear.

"I can and I do."

She dropped his hand abruptly as though it had burned her and rose to her feet. Standing with her hands clasped, she glanced at him warily, then down at her hands. Suddenly she began to laugh. "Would you look at me. I'm wringing my hands like the tragic heroine of a Victorian novel." As he opened his mouth to speak, she turned away and said urgently, "Don't say anything else right now. I've got to think. This is all wrong."

Walking around the bed, she tried to sort everything out, but the events of the evening kept colliding in her brain, leaving a confused mess. "Mr. Simons," she said finally, her voice vague and distracted.

Jerking his head up abruptly, he pinned her

with the sharpness of his look. "What about him?" he asked, his voice stiff.

"I was there," she whispered helplessly. "Outside your studio. I heard . . ." She stopped, unable to continue.

Drawing in a short, raspy breath, Dan moved swiftly to stand beside her, letting his arms fall as she backed away from him. His voice was painfully hoarse as he said, "God, babe, I'm sorry. If I had known, I would have shut him up."

"What he said didn't matter," she said tightly. "Oh, it hurt. That kind of thing will always hurt, but I can handle it. I always have." She closed her eyes and continued in a harsh whisper. "It was you, Dan. You looked so embarrassed, so . . . *ashamed.*" Covering her mouth with a hand that trembled, she leaned against the wall, feeling that she was at the end of her emotional capacity. She was ready for it to be over. Ready for the hurt to stop.

He reached out and jerked her upright, his fingers cutting painfully into her shoulders. "And you thought it was because of you?" he asked, his voice rough with anger. He gave her a short, hard shake. "It was for him!" Shaking her again, he repeated, "I was embarrassed for him . . . ashamed for him. He's a very dignified, very conservative . . . very nice man, but he let his personal problems swamp him and he was making a fool of himself in public." Releasing her abruptly, he turned away, running his long fingers through his hair in exasperation. "The whole ugly mess didn't even have anything to do with you. I knew what it was all about and I let him go. If I had known you were anywhere near that room, I wouldn't have let him continue."

He sat down heavily on the bed and sighed—a

sad, weary sound. "Come and sit down, Arlie. Let me explain."

He had her complete attention now and as she joined him on the bed, the iron bands around her chest eased, allowing her to breathe more freely.

He drew her back with him to lean against the headboard and rested his head on hers as he spoke. "Marshall Simon is a lot like your father was, Arlie. Nicer, but with the same misguided standards. He's a pillar of the community. A deacon in the church. All the things that go with that sort of life." He paused for a moment, then said quietly, "His son was arrested last week for dealing drugs."

Jerking her head away, she whispered in disbelief, "A pusher?"

He nodded. "The drugs would have been bad enough, but he was selling them. And some of his customers were just kids. It almost killed Marshall."

"I can see what it would do to him, Dan. But what does it have to do with me? I've never had anything to do with drugs. I don't even like to take aspirin."

"It *doesn't* have anything to do with you. I told you that. But you have to consider his state of mind. Remember how your father reacted when you misbehaved. He blamed it on the 'bad blood' you had inherited from your biological father. Anything to keep from admitting that it was his fault for neglecting you." Dan shrugged. "It was the same with Marshall. He had to find a scapegoat. He needed someone to blame so he wouldn't have to admit he had made a bad job of raising his son."

"I've never even met his son," she protested in confusion.

"No, but there was a woman in his life. A beautiful, frivolous little rich girl. Marshall blames her for getting his son involved in drugs," he explained. "Even given the external similarities, he probably wouldn't have transferred his antagonism—his hatred—to you if it hadn't been for a column in the paper."

"What column?" she asked in bewilderment.

"A gossip column. It had a paragraph about a French attorney—a man named Freneau—who was arrested outside a New York nightclub for possession of cocaine."

"But what . . ." she began in confusion, then stopped abruptly. "Freneau?" She looked at him sharply as suspicion crept into her mind. "Jean-Claude?" she whispered. When he nodded silently, she drew a breath and continued. "I still don't see what this has to do with me. Why should Mr. Simon read an article about a man I barely know and automatically transfer the antagonism he felt for some unknown female to me? Unless reading about the drugs set him off and I just happened to get in the way."

"I'm afraid there was more to it than that." He tightened his hold on her shoulder. "Your name was mentioned in the column."

She stared at him for a moment in uncomprehending silence, then sagged slowly in defeat. "You knew about it?" she asked wearily.

He nodded. "It was in yesterday's paper."

"Why didn't you tell me?" she asked, her voice dull.

"I knew you were trying to get away from the gossip," he said quietly. "I didn't want it to hurt you."

"What did it say about me?"

Leaning across her, he opened the bottom drawer of the nightstand and pulled out a folded newspaper, handing it to her in silence.

It was a typical gossip column. Arlie had read

thousands like it, many containing ridiculously magnified information and speculation about herself. She had always laughed at them, but she wasn't laughing now.

It told the story of Jean-Claude's arrest in an offhand way, making light of the whole story. Then below it in a separate paragraph, was a for-your-information notation about the divorce and return to Texas of the vivacious Arlie Fleming who had until recently been the constant companion of the aforementioned Paris attorney.

She laughed harshly. "We went to the same parties. And I haven't even seen him at a party in over six months." She let the newspaper drift to the floor. "But that doesn't matter, does it?"

"He knew he was wrong, Arlie," Dan said gently. "Before he left he apologized. He would have been very distressed if he had known that you overheard what he said. He went a little crazy. When he read that column, it was like reading about his son, including the involvement of a beautiful woman. He laid it all on you, but by the time he left he knew he was wrong about you. I think maybe he's beginning to realize he was wrong to blame anyone other than his son . . . and himself."

"I'm glad he's accepting it," she said slowly. "And I can understand his state of mind, but there was something else he said that wasn't caused by temporary madness. It was true. Everyone has been talking about me. When Eric and I got back with the gin and ice, you could have cut the tension in the living room with a knife." She smiled grimly. "They all thought we were necking in the kitchen."

"And that bothers you?"

"For me . . . no. Like I said, I can handle it. But it bothers me for you. You heard what he said. There are people who would use my reputation against you." Sliding from the bed, she sighed in resignation. "So nothing's changed. I still have to leave."

"This is why you decided you couldn't marry me?" he asked incredulously. "Because of some garbled facts thrown out by a sad old man?"

"It wasn't only him. Diane said . . ."

"I don't care if the prophet Elijah told you himself. It's garbage."

She hesitated, needing to hear the conviction in his voice, but still skeptical. Pulling distractedly at the tie of her robe, she muttered, "Well, if it had been the prophet Elijah, I probably wouldn't have believed him. Isn't he the one who fed children to bears?" She shook her head. "Or maybe that was Elisha . . . anyway it doesn't matter. What does matter is that Diane is a part of your world, Dan. She knows."

"She knows nothing!" he said, his voice raised in frustration. He pulled her back to the bed and continued in a quieter tone. "Look . . . Diane is a nice lady. But she's also a very misguided lady if she thinks your reputation can harm my career."

"She didn't exactly say *my* reputation," Arlie admitted slowly.

"So she said something general and your warped little brain added the rest. That's stupid, Arlie."

"But you said yourself that the Prescotts are conservative. You warned me about them when I first arrived," she reminded him. "And what about the way you always left me at home when you had business dinners and how you refused to let anyone come here?"

Dan's face reddened suddenly and he looked away, avoiding her eyes. He laughed shortly. "I was pretty obvious, wasn't I? I knew you were suspicious, but believe me I never dreamed you would interpret my behavior in that way." He rubbed his jaw ruefully, then looked into her eyes. "The reason for all those stupid things was Eric." He laughed again as he saw the astonishment in her eyes. "Didn't I tell you what I feel is too close to obsession for comfort? Eric was at those dinner parties. And most of those calls were from him. Once I started the lie by telling him I was too busy for company, I had to continue it with all my friends."

"But why?"

"For the same reason I warned you about behaving yourself right after you met him. I could tell you liked him and I was jealous."

"There was never anything like that between us," she said, then when she saw his raised eyebrows, she added, "Okay, I admit I thought maybe we could get something going later, but I never felt anything for him. And after you and I made love, I forgot about him completely."

"Maybe you didn't feel anything then, but you said yourself that you didn't know how you would react now that you're no longer a virgin." He shrugged. "Eric's attractive and more your type. I didn't want to take any chances."

"There was no chance," she murmured, but he was already going ahead with his explanation and didn't hear the softly spoken words.

"You were so confident that you wanted to marry me, I thought it was time I took a chance on allowing him back into your life and, besides that, I wanted all my friends to meet you. You were right. I did know about the gossip, but I knew that when they met you—got to know you— they couldn't help but love you and see the basic honesty inside you."

"God, were you ever wrong," she muttered.

"No, I was right," he said firmly. "Didn't you see them? They came here ready to pick you to pieces in their heads and they left here dazzled, never knowing what hit them." He chuckled, hugging her close. "You could charm the socks off an Eskimo. And I never doubted it for a minute."

"You invited them here for me?" she gasped.

"Of course. I knew you were worried about the gossip and I wanted to show you that it didn't matter. They may still believe there was some truth to the rumors, but now that they've met you, they don't care. They know you could never do anything vicious or cruel and that's what matters to most people. There may be a few diehards, but you'll bring them around eventually." He tilted her chin, his eyes shining with love as he looked deep into her eyes. "I have faith in you, babe."

She closed her eyes weakly, finally allowing the knowledge of his love to wash over her in warm, vibrant waves. There was just one more thing they had to clear up before she gave in to it completely. "Dan, about Diane . . ."

"Is something else she said bothering you?"

"Not exactly," she said hesitantly, then the words came out in a rush. "Dan, she's perfect for you. She's knowledgeable, attractive, and she has no questionable past. I know she cares for you and . . ." she stared up at the ceiling, ". . . that first day you said it could have been serious if she hadn't been interested in someone else." Cutting her eyes back to his face, she said softly, "I don't think she would be interested in anyone if she thought she had a chance with you."

"That's not exactly what I said." Tilting her face, he brushed a kiss across her cheek to the corner of her mouth. "I said we drifted into being just friends, *then* she became interested in someone else. I like Diane, Arlie. I've always liked her, but I don't love her. I couldn't."

"Couldn't?"

Unconsciously, he began to caress the side of her neck with one large hand as he stared unseeingly ahead. "I couldn't," he murmured, "because once, a long time ago when the moon was blue, I fell in love with an irritating pest of a girl . . ." he shrugged helplessly, ". . . and I just never fell out again."

She sucked in her breath sharply, feeling weak, giddy. "Way back then?" she whispered in wonder.

"Back then?" he laughed, softly mocking himself. "I loved you the minute I set eyes on you. More than that, I wanted you to belong to me." He leaned his head back against the headboard, his fingers continuing the gentle massage of her neck and shoulder. "When I pulled you out of the hedge with your hair all in tangles and your bare feet carrying enough dirt to plant a rose garden, you looked up at me like you were a queen confronting a forward peasant. There was such life in your eyes! You were a courageous, outrageous, *vibrant* little monster. You would steal apples from Mr. Fenster's tree just to see if you could get away with it, then turn around and carry an injured dog a mile so that I could give it first aid for you."

He looked down at her, his dark eyes telling her as much as his words. "You belonged to me a long time before we made love. Your laugh, your fire, got in my blood and made you a part of me. Then, that night in the gazebo, I found out I wanted a lot more than your laugh. You were eighteen and innocent and I wanted you naked and beneath me." His lips twisted in a grim smile. "I felt like the lowest kind of worm for letting it go as far as it did. And what I did to you later in my dreams . . . God! I couldn't look you in the eye for weeks after that."

"I remember," she laughed shakily. "I was kicking myself, too. I thought you were avoiding me because you didn't care about me in that way. That you were ashamed for letting yourself get carried away."

"Oh, I was ashamed all right, but not for that reason. I cared in every way it was possible to care, but you weren't ready for that kind of thing and it was my responsibility to make you stop and think."

"I wish you had forgotten your responsibility for once," she said wryly. "Because I *was* ready for that kind of thing. I thought you were the one who didn't want our relationship to change directions. So . . ." she said in a sigh, "I squelched the way I felt about you. I buried it so deeply inside me, it was hidden even from myself. Even when we made love I didn't recognize it for what it was. I simply knew that the thought of making love to someone else felt wrong." She looked up at him, parting her lips to say the words, but he placed his hand on her mouth, preventing her from speaking.

"Arlie, you are the most loving person I've ever known," he said in a harsh whisper. "But, please, babe, don't say it if you don't mean it . . . *really* mean it. I'll settle for what you can give me. I'll be your friend or your lover or both. But whatever our relationship is, I want it to be based on truth."

Looking down, she slowly opened her hands and his eyes followed hers to the cuts on her palms. "I thought I was going to have to leave you," she said simply.

He closed his eyes, expelling his breath in a harsh, raspy sigh, and leaned his forehead against hers as he whispered, "Then say it, Arlie."

"I love you," she murmured. "In that special way . . . the forever kind of way." She lifted her hand to touch the golden bird resting on his chest.

"I thought you were ready to have the weight of both of us off your neck."

"Never," he groaned, then slid her body down until she lay on the bed beneath him. As he lowered his lips to meet hers, he whispered urgently, "Never," the word a promise for the future.

Arlie unclipped the dry photographs, stacking them as she went, then sat down to enjoy the fruits of her labor. She had taken the pictures at Dan's forty-sixth birthday party, but had only today found the time to develop them.

The first was a group portrait. Her brood. She smiled, feeling again the fullness of her life. Would she never get over the wonder of having her own family? Even when they were at their most argumentative, she still found herself smiling in satisfaction at the noise.

She went slowly over each figure in the picture. Dan, trying so hard to look serious when she knew he was laughing at the smear of icing on her new silk blouse. Next, eleven-year-old Steve, named for his uncle but looking so much like his father. Then came the twins, Michael and Peter. Nine years old and double the trouble. Prospective scientists both. They never stopped asking questions about things others took for granted. And last, at six years of age, the baby of the family— Ammie.

Arlie chuckled at the look in her daughter's eyes as she laid the photograph aside and picked up the next one. It was of Dan alone and she caught her breath at the look in his eyes. He wasn't suppressing laughter in this picture. He was gazing at her with the love and desire that was always present in his eyes. Having four children called for a lot of self-restraint. They could no longer make love every time a glance or a movement sparked their passion, but it was worth the wait. And each time they came together, it was with a hunger that was fresh and new.

Dan had given her so much through the years. Not just four children and the security of a family. He had given her the security of his love. And while he had taken on some of her spontaneity, from him, she had learned restraint.

And from him, Arlie had learned to cry. In her hospital room, the day after Steve was born, when Dan had lifted the tiny, sleeping baby in his large, awkward looking hands and looked down at him with such a wealth of pride and love and awe . . . she had cried. She had laughed with relief and cried with love, both at the same time. Dan had rocked her in his arms, laughing with her . . . crying with her . . . understanding how much the moment meant to her. The doctors had tried to tell them it was simply a case of postpartum depression, but Arlie knew they were wrong. For the first time in her life she was secure enough to let all her emotions surface . . . and to cry.

She touched the glossy photograph gently, wishing it were night and the children were asleep in bed. His dear face didn't seem to have changed at all in the last twelve years. Maybe there were wrinkles and gray hairs, but all she could see was the love that remained the same.

"You should be ashamed of yourself," she muttered, laying the picture aside. "Only truly depraved women lust after married men." She looked slowly through the remaining pictures. Dan— blowing out a forest fire of candles. The boys— fighting to see who would help her cut the cake. Ammie—stealing a bite of ice cream instead of dishing it onto her brother's plate. All so precious. All because of Dan.

Suddenly her idyl was interrupted by the sound

of breaking glass and she laid aside the photographs to walk quickly out of the darkroom into the bedroom. But before she could reach the hallway to investigate, Dan walked in carrying an extremely suspicious looking baseball.

"Again?" she sighed in resignation.

"Again," he confirmed. "It landed right in the middle of my drawing board. I shudder to think what would have happened if I had been sitting there." His eyes were shining with laughter, but his lips were firm and his voice stern as he continued. "What are we going to do with her?"

Moving closer, she put her arms around his neck. "Don't worry about her. She'll be fine." She rubbed her face against his neck and her voice dropped to a soft murmur. "After all, she has you."

He glanced down at her skeptically, then, seeing the look on her face, a fire began to kindle in his eyes and he dipped his head to capture her lips. But the kiss had barely begun when they heard shouts from the yard below and together they walked to the window.

Looking down, they got a glimpse of mischievous violet eyes, an unrepentant grin, and a flash of bare feet before Ammie turned the corner with her brothers in hot pursuit.

Dan chuckled and pulled her close. "You're right. She'll be fine."

Then, knowing it would be quite a while before the boys caught up with their cunning sister, they walked arm in arm to the bed.

THE SHAMROCK TRINITY

60 Minutes to a Better, More Beautiful You!

Now it's easier than ever to awaken your sensuality, stay slim forever—even make yourself irresistible. With Bantam's bestselling subliminal audio tapes, you're only 60 minutes away from a better, more beautiful you!

__ 45004-2	**Slim Forever**	$8.95
__ 45112-X	**Awaken Your Sensuality**	$7.95
__ 45035-2	**Stop Smoking Forever**	$8.95
__ 45130-8	**Develop Your Intuition**	$7.95
__ 45022-0	**Positively Change Your Life**	$8.95
__ 45154-5	**Get What You Want**	$7.95
__ 45041-7	**Stress Free Forever**	$8.95
__ 45106-5	**Get a Good Night's Sleep**	$7.95
__ 45094-8	**Improve Your Concentration**	$7.95
__ 45172-3	**Develop A Perfect Memory**	$8.95

THE LATEST IN BOOKS
AND AUDIO CASSETTES